Advance Praise for *Squirming All the Way Up*

"*Squirming All_____ torn apart by religious extr_____ masterfully crafts a cosmic ._____ror, gore, heart, and worm_____

—Angela S_____ author of
Frost Bite

"*Squirming All the Way Up* is a fun yet important horror book for our times. With his direct prose and clever storytelling, Joey Powell offers us here not only a book you won't be able to put down but also a tale to keep you up at night wishing the bigots in your life could be dewormed."

—J.V. Gachs, author of *Epiphany* and *Unholy*

"A frank, unapologetic, visceral, and gross look at some of the really monstrous shit that is happening to us as a country right now. The All-Father is one of the coolest monsters I've seen in a long time."

—T.T. Madden, author of *The Cosmic Color*

"Thought-provoking, culturally relevant, and straight up nasty in all the right ways. Joey Powell gives us unforgiving horrors that only get nastier as they unravel, promising to still be writhing in your brain long after."

—David Washburn, author of DIY Exorcism

SQUIRMING ALL THE WAY UP

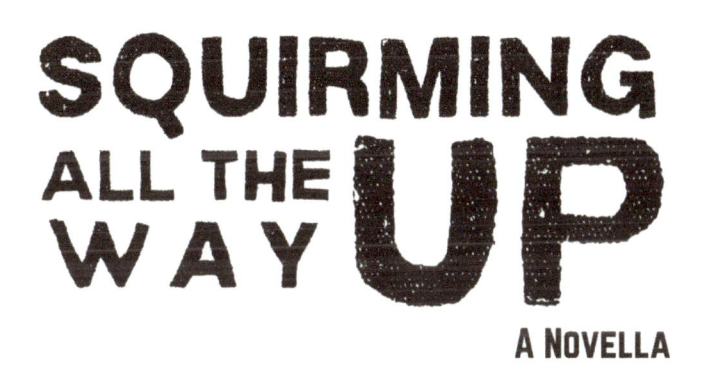

A NOVELLA

JOEY POWELL

Content Warning:

Religious trauma, homophobia, transphobia, transition therapy, deadnaming, discussions of abortion

Madness Heart Press
2006 Idlewilde Run Dr.
Austin, Texas 78744

This is a work of fiction. Names, characters, places, and incidents either are the product of the author's imagination or are used fictitiously. Any resemblance to actual persons, living or dead, events, or locales is entirely coincidental.

Copyright © 2025 Joey Powell
Cover & Interior Design by Joey Powell
Edited by Lisa Tone

All rights reserved. No part of this book may be reproduced or used in any manner without written permission of the copyright owner except for the use of quotations in a book review. For more information, address: john@madnessheart.press

First Edition
Print ISBN: 978-1-955745-97-0
Digital ISBN: 978-1-955745-98-7
madnessheart.press

To those who believe they are superior.

May you never find peace.

SQUIRMING ALL THE WAY UP

CHAPTER ONE

Fifty-Seven Minutes After Deworming

There are many things Joe Sanderson wished to say to his brother, but every time he talked, it felt like a knife spun around in his gut. If he were stronger and if pints of blood weren't pouring out of his side and onto the gurney, he would admit a thousand times that it was all a lie. He would curse the year-and-change of his life he wasted avoiding Anthony.

As Joe lay there, feeling sorry for himself and maybe taking his final breaths, he remembered that he never told Anthony he didn't know about the worms.

Anthony, I didn't know about the goddamn worms, he thought, trying to form the words on his lips. Every time he did, his jaw seemingly yanked on an invisible hook connected to the open flesh.

Maybe he just didn't want to see what was in plain view. But isn't that faith in a nutshell? Belief in the things one can't see despite the things they can?

Goddamn worms.

In a way, Anthony saved Joe from himself, because all of this started with a call.

Well—to be more specific—it started a few days ago with their mother dying.

Five Days Before Deworming

Joe had fallen asleep after another unromantic love-making session with his wife. He'd known since shortly after they'd met that Darla wore wigs, but she never allowed him to see her without one. When they made love, the wig shifted slightly but mostly stayed put because, well, there wasn't a whole lot of movement going on. Sex had become a utilitarian performance. After joining the Fellowship of the First Divine, Joe understood that the purpose of his pairing with Darla was to procreate. At least, that's what she said she heard when God spoke to her.

Goddamn worms.

He didn't much mind that the sex was bad because Darla had rescued him from the darkest moment in his life, a hole he never thought he'd be able to crawl out of. Unbeknownst to him at the time, he'd traded in one addiction for another.

The weak orgasm that night precluded a nightmare of a world in ruin. An old woman screamed as she burned to death. Joe didn't immediately recognize her as his mother. She was too far away, and all he could see was a flailing set of arms.

In the dream, he didn't question how he'd gotten to the open field or why there was smoke everywhere or how the old woman managed to catch fire. Dreams are weird like that. When you're in them, everything just ... is.

He ran closer toward hers as the white hair on either side of her head caught flames. It was then, with her face lit in the orange dance of fire, that he recognized her. She was older than he remembered. After so many years without contact, her face had dropped out of his memory. Still, he'd recognize that face anywhere—even in a dream.

And in this dream, one he'd had dozens of times on dozens of nights, there was no saving her.

Maybe that's the point, he remembered thinking in his dream state. *Maybe that's what God's trying to show me.*

A sound like a muffled foghorn blasted, vibrating the ground as if from an instrument embedded deep inside the earth.

His mother kept flailing in the fire, reminding him of one of those dancing inflatable things in front of a car dealership with the big eyes and painted-on smile, except her eyes were scared and the skin around her mouth was bubbling.

Her arms stopped flailing and instead reached through the fire with her hands spread open.

Whatever she was trying to say came out gargled like the last remaining ounces of water in her charring body had collected in her throat.

He was the only one around. The only one who could help. It was his divine purpose to help her as so many others had helped him so frequently before. But as soon as he leaned forward, the weight he should have felt at the fronts of his feet was nonexistent.

He was off the ground and floating.

His mother's eyes popped into white, slimy bits. Her vocal cords exploded in a final scream. Small clusters like honeycombs appeared in her eye sockets, expanding beyond what her bone structure would accept. With sharp cracks of bone, the clusters expanded into charcoal-black fingers, forcing their way through her eye sockets.

He rose off the ground, the gravity of the dreamworld slowly abandoning him. He reached for her but was powerless to control his ascension.

The black hands came out, their knuckles ripping through skull and skin. Her shrieks subsided, and everything that remained of her, including the foreign hands, was coated in flames.

In the stormy darkness that surrounded Joe, several other limp bodies floated as well. As he went higher, his view of the world expanded. More fires became visible, and within them, others like his mother were condemned to burn for as long as their bodies could bear it.

He looked down at his feet as they slowly moved away from that burning mess of wet skin that just seconds ago had looked like Mom. The arms from her eyes clawed toward him, their flesh melted down to the bone.

Rolling dark clouds, thick and angry, blanketed the sky, with flashes of lightning casting bursts of brightness in the spaces between them, forcing a monstrous sight into his vision.

A bundle of giant, wide, boneless appendages, shining with slick skin, squirming in wave-like movements behind the storm, drew him closer to its orbit.

Four Days Before Deworming

Sunlight touched Joe's face. He slowly opened his eyes, convincing himself he was no longer floating.

His dresser came into view, as did the Holy Bible on top of it and the lamp that had kept it illuminated the night before.

The other side of the bed was smooth, with a sequence of decorative pillows stacked from the headboard through the first quarter-length of the mattress. Darla, being a morning person, usually got up before Joe. He was prone to read the Good Book well into the late hours of the night, whereas she enjoyed her Bible study in the morning.

Joe looked down at the foot of the bed and pulled back the comforter and the bedsheet. His feet were matted with dried dirt, leaving muddy stains on the fabric surrounding them.

Sleepwalking again.

He rubbed his face and willed himself up to his feet, hearing the faintest hissing sound from the floorboards underneath the bed. Joe had warned Darla of snakes in their crawlspace for the past four months. They'd had a member of the church come down to inspect it a few weeks ago, but they claimed they couldn't find anything. Joe was too chicken-shit to check himself.

Joe headed to the bathroom to clean up. When he got in front of the mirror, he noticed a red circle on his right shoulder bleeding through his shirt. It flared up every time he had the dream. His skin was raised around it, blue in the middle like a suction cup had had its way with him. He had gone to see a doctor a few months prior when he started getting the mark, and they wrote it off as a "blood deposit" that came as a result of his alcohol detox.

And that was a good enough explanation for Joe.

A muffled Christian tune played behind the bedroom door as Joe threw on a t-shirt and jeans, but he could make out most of the words. Something about a guy thanking God for saving him.

He went out to the hallway and pulled open the sliding doors to the washer and dryer, sitting side-by-side in a space just big enough for both of them. He threw the bedsheet in the washer but knew better than to start it while Darla wasn't watching. Such tasks were the responsibility of the woman, she liked to remind him. All he needed to do was focus on providing. He never felt like he was providing much, though. Outside of the monthly payment for his truck and utilities, they didn't have much in the way of financial burden since the house was paid for by Darla's family. He guessed that's why she accepted him as a simple day laborer. No fancy job and no real ladder to climb.

The responsibilities thing never completely sat right with him. Joe and his brother, Anthony, grew up with their mom and each other and no one else. They were forced into a state of self-sufficiency. Joe knew how to do laundry. He knew how to cook. But Darla insisted—no, *demanded*—that he let her handle all of it.

Darla was eleven years younger than Joe, but her being in her 20s and Joe being in his 30s didn't drive too much of a wedge between them. She wasn't social media obsessed like so many other girls Joe had met on dating apps before her and before he had found his place in the Fellowship of the First Divine. In fact, the only obsession she had was for the Lord, and that was something she and Joe had in common.

A squeaky voice bounced over the Christian soft rock tune from the living room. It was met with a cheeky giggle—the type that Darla would give when she was genuinely happy.

The music got louder as he walked down the hallway, which split into the kitchen and the living room. Darla cooked breakfast with a towel over her shoulder, bobbing to the music. Bacon and eggs sizzled in a skillet. To Joe, the smell was absolutely divine. She flipped the bacon with a pair of tongs, then noticed Joe standing in the hallway opening.

"Good mornin'," she said with the same delicate smile that made Joe want to be a better person a year and a half ago.

A high-pitched country drawl addressed Joe from the kitchen table. "Mornin', son."

Father Castor sat in one of their wooden chairs, one leg over the other, blowing on the surface of a steaming cup of coffee. He had the look of a fifteen-year-old boy with a freshly-sprouted mustache. Blemishes cast a red constellation all over his pasty white face, the hormones from his adolescence still circulating through him at the ripe age of twenty-two, but his receding hairline was like a promise of the old man he'd be one day. Twenty-two and the kid was already going bald. Genetics can be a bit cruel like that.

In the three months that Castor had been placed in an apprenticeship position to be the successor of the Fellowship's head pastor, Joe had never gotten used to this boy calling him "son."

"Hi there, Castor—uh—Father Castor." It was a slip-up that Joe had intended, and it was worth it to see the smile fade from Castor's face just for a moment.

"Father Castor and I were just discussing the town fair this weekend," Darla said. "He's trying to rally members of the Fellowship to participate."

"It's not too late to get a booth," Father Castor said confidently.

"I was telling him that to participate would be to endorse the City Council, and, well ... you know how I feel about the City Council." Darla lifted the tongs again and rearranged the bacon. "Not only do they discriminate against the church, but they made the decision to have the fair on a Sunday. That's as clear a slap in the face to the Fellowship as I've ever seen one."

The discrimination she was referring to was a local ordinance in circulation that would make it illegal for the church to only hire or admit members whom they deemed fit the Fellowship's "mission." It was no secret what those ideal members looked like.

"And I was just telling Darla that our numbers are dwindling," Father Castor said. "Sure, we have members of the younger generations in our ranks, but they can only do so much to spread the word of God. What we need is recruitment on a larger scale. What do you think, Joe?" Castor took a sip of coffee, smiling at Joe as he gulped it down.

"Um …" Joe didn't have much capacity to think at that point. Part of him was still living in the nightmare, rattled by the writhing creature in the sky.

"Oh, what am I sayin'?" Castor stood up from his chair. "The gentleman just woke up. I'm gonna let y'all have the mornin' to yourselves." He turned to Darla, holding up the mug. "Mind if I take this with me?"

Darla waved the greasy pair of tongs in his direction. "I know where to find ya, Father." She began transferring bacon from the skillet to a plate.

Castor gave Joe a nod and a raise of his mug, then walked out the front door and closed it behind him. It was very un-Christian-like of Joe, but he imagined himself chucking the young pastor across the room. Father Castor had a way of getting under Joe's skin. Maybe it was the way Joe was obligated to call him "Father." Maybe it was the always-chipper demeanor. Maybe Joe just wished he'd been that confident and self-realized ten years ago.

"Hey, uh … Did you feel me get up last night?" Joe asked Darla.

"You know I'm a hard sleeper, honey. An earthquake couldn't wake me."

"Hm …" He felt an itch on his shoulder—exposed skin scabbing over—and rubbed it.

"Somethin' botherin' you?"

"Nah, just … didn't sleep well is all."

"Why don't you sit? I got coffee on the burner."

Joe sat at the kitchen table and waited on the mug. He never asked Darla to bring him food and coffee, she just did it. It was a different kind of love than he was used to.

He never imagined he'd be able to come home after a hard day of labor to a freshly cooked meal, that he'd be able to stare out through the long glass pane just beyond the edge of the table at a view of the woods, reminding himself that it all actually belonged to Darla and him. He and Anthony didn't have all that much growing up, and at this point in his life—equipped with a mental checklist of all the wrong things a man can do—Joe wasn't sure he deserved it.

The TV was playing the local news, which was a bit overkill since Darla had the music so high, but he watched the moving images all the same, trying to replace the sights from the dream still prominent in his mind. Darla set a coffee mug on the table in front of him

"Thank you, dear," he said.

She touched his shoulder—the one with the mark—before going back to the stovetop.

"You startin' work late today?" Darla called out from the kitchen.

"Yeah, I gotta make a few stops before," Joe said.

"Where ya goin'?"

He took a sip of his coffee. Strong, black, hot, lighting his pallet on fire. "Just makin' a few stops."

She let out that same cute giggle loud enough for him to hear it. "Men and their secrets."

It was those types of comments that made Joe wonder if Darla was a much older woman pretending to be twenty-two. So far as Joe knew, he was her only love.

"I'm not keepin' secrets," he said.

"All the better. Men need secrets to make 'em feel all independent and whatnot. Women, well ... we *tell* secrets. Makes us feel included."

SQUIRMING ALL THE WAY UP

Darla brought him a plate, arranging it to the left of his coffee mug. Bubbles of grease slid down the bacon, mixing into the eggs.

"Fix a plate and eat with me," Joe told her.

"This mess ain't gonn' clean itself, now is it?"

He chuckled at that and turned his attention back to the TV screen. A youngish guy in a suit with a stiff haircut, probably around Joe's age, talked right at him as a square image popped up in the left-hand corner of the screen. In the image, a pale teenager with blond shoulder-length hair posed for a yearbook picture with a crooked smile slightly raised on one side. It was someone he recognized. He leaned forward, trying to evade the stereo and replace it with the dapper newsman's voice. "And the search is ongoing for Trisha McCann, sixteen years old. Trisha was reported missing a week ago today ..."

Without turning to Darla, he asked, "Elle McCann's daughter's been missing?"

"Daughter?" Darla said back.

He gave Darla a curious look, then a wave of uncontrollable congestion clouded his head like nails swirling under his scalp. Loud, rage-filled voices reminding him what Trisha McCann used to be. Every Sunday, Elle McCann's sister Diane asked the congregation to pray for her "nephew Tristan," who had been tempted by Satan's confusion and "decided" he was a different gender.

Correct yourself, Joe, he heard himself think. The voice was his own, but the thought was from something else.

"Right, Elle McCann's son," Joe said. "Don't you think we should go out lookin' for him?"

"I trust that God is lookin' out for him. And God will see to it that he's brought back safely."

JOEY POWELL

"Maybe it's God's punishment," Joe said. *Good, Joe. That's good.* "Tristan's lived this lie long enough, and he's now facing righteous retribution."

Darla smiled. "Yes, I trust that God has a plan for that boy."

Joe told himself that when he prayed that night, he'd be praying for one of God's creations to return home safely. Not a girl or boy, but a child of God.

A child damned that can be saved.

It was hard for Joe to admit that he'd been seeing things that weren't really there. He used to do drugs and see all sorts of wild shit, but what he'd been experiencing since he got sober was different. It felt like all the drugs and alcohol detoxed from his blood were out there in the air, whispering for him to take them back. He thought prayer would make the hallucinations go away, but it didn't.

A raspy cry tickled his ear, soft at first, but unmistakably coming from the woods. Joe looked out past the intersecting tree limbs, where a woman stood barefoot under the shade of the trees. The thin fabric of her white nightgown danced loosely in the light summer breeze, as did her brown hair, which covered the entirety of her face like a veil. The awful cries came from her chest, where she held a baby in a red blanket.

Red streaks crawled down the woman's nightgown as the child screamed, becoming thicker and thicker, until a puddle of bloody viscera formed around the woman's feet.

SQUIRMING ALL THE WAY UP

Joe stepped down from the porch, trying to blink the woman away, but she remained in his vision, dangling like an ornament through twisted branches, her cold, expressionless face refusing to leave his sight. He knew he'd see her again, just like he'd seen others several times over.

A collection of ghosts haunting his restless mind.

Something shifted in Father Castor's skull. Joe could have sworn he saw it.

A small bulge stretched the bare skin at the top of Father Castor's receding hairline. "Everything all right up there, Father?" Joe said, sitting in a pew of the church of the Fellowship of the First Divine. A fresh coat of paint wafted from the stark white wood, its A-frame coming to a high point on the ceiling.

"What do you mean?" Father Castor replied as the lump disappeared from his skin.

Joe stammered. "Looked like, uh ... I don't know how to say this. It ... looked like somethin' in your head ... moved."

Father Castor gave him a dumb, puzzled kind of look.

"Yeah, like, uh ..." *A baby's hand moving in a pregnant belly*, he wanted to say, but thought the better of it.

Father Castor's jaw came up and formed a smile. "Don't poke fun at my hairline, now."

Castor was old-school-Southern and naturally left the "w" off of "now."

JOEY POWELL

Joe had come to see Father Henry, a man he had come to see as a father figure, but instead would have to settle for the pastor's young protege, a scrawny kid who enjoyed sipping coffee out of *his* mug and talking to *his* wife while Joe slept.

Come on now, Joe thought. *This is a man of God.*

Father Castor stood with his hands in front of his slim stomach, fingers interlocked, the sleeves of his black robe dangling from his wrists. "Now, where were we?" he said as he walked down the velvet rug separating the two columns of pews. "Right. Your recurring dream. When you hear the phrase 'God spoke to me,' what does that mean to you?"

When Joe was a child, he imagined a booming, mythic voice calling down to him from the Heavens. He spent years wondering when he would hear that awesome sound. The Bible, indeed, has several examples of God speaking to His disciples, so why not Joe?

"These dreams you have," Father Castor said, "they occur multiple times a week, yes?"

"Yessir," Joe said. "It starts with me wanderin' around a field. I see someone burnin' in a fire, and then I just kinda ... float up."

"Into Heaven, I'm guessin'?"

"It seems that way in the dreams. It's like ... I understand in my heart that's what's happenin', but when I look up at the sky—"

"Is it not possible that God speaks to us so frequently, but in a language we simply can't comprehend? Is it possible that God speaks to us every day, several times a day even, and we miss it? We as children of God must keep our eyes open to the language of God. When he beckons, do not ignore his call."

"Do you actually believe God is callin' on me?"

"Why is that so difficult to imagine?"

"Because the thing I see in the sky, it's not really the image of God I had in my head."

Father Castor stopped pacing. The facade of the showman was broken, and a sudden look that might have been concern or intrigue struck him. "What is it you see?"

Joe hesitated before releasing the words from his tongue. "Somethin' monstrous. Somethin' thick and squirming like a massive cluster of snakes or somethin' slidin' all over each other."

Father Castor took a long breath in and out, then made his way back to Joe and sat. "You describe this being as monstrous. Maybe instead think of it as somethin' beautiful. Think of it as the way God has chosen to reveal Himself to you." He slapped Joe's leg. "Think of this as an exciting time, Joseph. If I had to interpret what you've seen in your dreams, I'd say the people in the fire need your help. I'd say they're beggin' you to take them with ya toward the light."

Letting go of Castor's annoying insistence on calling him *Joseph*, it was exactly what Joe needed to hear. All Joe wanted was for the nightmares to *mean* something. Joe had known his mother needed saving. Growing up, Andrea Sanderson was all Joe and his brother had. When Anthony revealed to the family that he was living an un-Godly lifestyle, Joe and his mother didn't know what to do. Send him away to a camp to be treated? Keep it secret? How could they when Anthony was plastering his filth and sin all over the internet, dressing in rainbow colors and waving pride flags in public like a proud heathen? When Joe's mother told members of their church about Anthony's homosexuality, they said under no circumstance could Anthony set foot in the same place they prayed. His mother struggled with that ultimatum a great deal. At first, Joe thought the struggle was due to the understanding that one of her children was living in unconscionable sin. But that wasn't it at all.

Joe's mother struggled with the church's response.

One Sunday morning, she decided not to go to church. She said she wasn't feeling well. But it seemed that she somehow didn't feel well just about every Sunday after that. Eventually, Joe confronted her about it. "Why?" he asked her. "Why do you refuse to go to church?"

She told him she refused the church because the church refused her son.

To Joe, Andrea Sanderson had turned her back on God. Sitting on that pew with Father Castor, he was now convinced that it was his purpose to bring God back into her life.

Father Castor asked Joe to pray with him. The pastor bowed his head, and Joe witnessed something shift again, rubbing against the interior of the young man's skin.

The sun hit Joe's skin hard as he ran lumber through a table saw. He was working a job at a nice suburban neighborhood where some wealthy couple was gutting their deck and replacing it with a new one. Sunspots had started forming on his arms, thanks in large part to the nine-hour shifts under ultraviolet radiation. The site manager, Marty, had encouraged him to wear long sleeves—that moisture-wicking stuff—but the summers kept getting hotter in Virginia, and it seemed like no amount of sunscreen could block those rays.

It was at that property while he was working with the guys and trying to get his mind off of the bumps moving along Father Castor's skull—questioning whether he'd actually seen anything at all—that he got a call on his flip phone. He took his gloves off and stepped away.

A woman's voice came on the other line, her tone direct and serious. "Hello, is this Joe Sanderson?" she asked.

"Yes, ma'am, it is," he responded.

"Mr. Sanderson, I'm calling regarding your mother, Andrea Sanderson. Do you have a moment to speak?"

"She all right?" Of course she wasn't. When has anyone gotten a call from a random stranger to let them know their mom was doing gangbusters?

Joe drove away from the job site and through the neighborhood, past pristine streets with thick trees sprouting branches that met in arches above him. He found a long, quiet road with a grassy shoulder to pull onto.

The tears came all at once.

He cried so much his eyes burned.

He cried until the last streaks of sunlight faded from the tops of trees that lined the road.

Hours had passed and his sobs were dry, as if his tear ducts and his body by extension had nothing left to give.

It wasn't until he forced himself to move, like a puppeteer pulling his own strings, that he realized Anthony had called. He imagined

Anthony handling the news better than he had. Anthony was always the more level-headed brother.

You could have saved her, he heard himself say. *She's burning. Burning. Burning.*

His mind screamed as if it, too, was on fire.

The headlights of Joe's truck landed on Darla as she stomped out the front door. For such a tiny woman, he could almost hear her feet slam against the ground like a sledgehammer on concrete as she went down the steps and onto the driveway.

"Where on Earth have you been, Joe?" she yelled. "Marty said you left the job site without sayin' a single word. You wouldn't answer your phone—not for him, not for me. What's goin' on with you?"

As soon as Joe stepped out of the truck, she was on him, her chest against his ribs, her nose pointed upward.

"Well?" She waited for an admission. Her nostrils flared as she took a couple whiffs of his mouth. "Joe, have you …" Her face shifted from rage to sadness. "No."

She darted past him and pulled open the driver's side door. It would have been hard for her to miss the twelve-pack of beer riding shotgun, torn open at the side, with four empty beer cans next to it. It was like he didn't even try to hide it from her, like he wanted her to catch him and tell him he had done wrong.

She turned back to Joe and hit the meaty part of his shoulder—the one without the mark—summoning what little force she had.

SQUIRMING ALL THE WAY UP

"After everything you've done, Joe? After *everything*?" Her eyes became glassy, forming strands of tears down her cheeks.

Joe wanted her to be mad at him. He wanted to be punished because that was something he could work through. He could do right by Darla and seek her forgiveness.

Joe thought at the time he was feeling sadness, but the tears were guilt. Guilt over shunning his family. Joe's mother wasn't around anymore to forgive him, and the weight of that thought was crushing him down into the bedrock of his existence while his mind tried to convince him she was trapped in eternal damnation.

"I need to tell you somethin'," he said.

Darla emptied the beer cans in the sink while Joe stood in the shower, his head dangling under the steaming cone of water as he cocooned himself in the droning sounds of wet pellets pounding at the floor of the tub.

The shadow of a human body appeared behind the shower curtain, breaking him from the solemn trance. A low weeping sound cut through the noise of the shower—light breaths, slow whimpers.

"What is it, Darla?" he said with a hand against the curtain.

The silent shadow stood there as he ripped the shower curtain open. It wasn't Darla on the other side.

It was his mother, her skin bubbling, steaming, her eyes two white puddles on her cheeks. She stared at him with black pits under her brows, sobbing, but without eyes to cry with.

Joe stumbled backward, slipping on the shower floor and catching his skin against the side and back of the shower, sliding downward with a sharp screeching sound.

With the water hitting his midsection, he looked back up.

His mother was no longer there.

Joe lay in bed that night with Darla spooning him. The thought of little Darla being big spoon to his little spoon would have made him laugh were he not so sad.

"I called Marty and told him you'll need to take some time," she said. "He was understanding."

"I can't stop workin', Darla," he told her.

"We'll be fine for a week or two."

He stayed silent for a while, then said, "Thanks, honey."

"For what?"

"For takin' care of me."

"This ain't the worst I've seen you, babe."

"Yeah ... Thanks for always takin' care of me is what I mean." He went silent again. This was what he liked most about Darla. She could keep a conversation going with anyone but was also generous in letting the quiet moments linger. "Do you think my mom's in ..." He didn't want to say it and make it true.

"Do I think she's in what?"

Having been sober for a year, the alcohol had kicked in fast, and it felt like stones were pressing his eyelids down.

Did Joe think she was in Hell?

He did.

He truly, wholeheartedly did.

The horns blasted, vibrating the same open field Joe had visited the night before. The shirt and boxers he'd fallen asleep in rippled in a warm smoke-ridden breeze, forcing gray tendrils into his lungs.

Fire sparked in the distance—about fifty yards across the flat land, sending a dozen arms of flame upward all at once. The screams came soon after.

He sprinted toward the fire, feeling warm mud mash against his bare feet.

As he came closer, he could start to make out a young man engulfed in flames reaching his hand out. Even though the sounds emitted from his mouth were high and shrill and cracking with a million needles of fire, Joe recognized the voice.

"Joe! Help me!" Anthony shouted with his arm moving over the fiery threshold. From elbow to shoulder, Anthony's skin grew welts.

His brother was more fire than human at that point, but dream-Joe thought he could pull him out. He didn't get a chance to, though. Before he was able to reach Anthony's hand, his feet lifted off the ground.

Even as Anthony's skin turned black and his face melted, lips peeling back toward his teeth like a sinkhole, Anthony continued to scream.

The sky creature wiggled behind dark clouds.

Joe's image of God pulling him closer.

JOEY POWELL

Joe woke up standing, facing the woods. His legs felt weak, shocked by the sudden weight of gravity, causing him to sink uncontrollably to the ground. The mud was wet against boxers, soaking through to his skin instantly.

A ball of soreness grew in his shoulder. He touched it and felt wet blood around the mark, and then something that wasn't blood around that—something gooey and viscous.

Something slithered behind him, prompting him to whip his head around.

A long shape danced on the ground, rapidly moving away from him, the small amount of moonlight above it forming the outline of a thick snake. It moved in the direction of the house—there one second, gone the next.

At the time, he just thought it was an extension of his dream, his consciousness catching up to his surroundings. His God sending him on a quest.

Joe Sanderson believed that God had called on him to save his mother right before she died. Now He was calling on Joe to save Anthony.

This time, he would heed the calling.

CHAPTER TWO

Forty-Seven Minutes After Deworming

It wasn't difficult for Anthony to think of an explanation as to why police officers carry pistols instead of semi-automatic rifles. Yes, Anthony was an anti-gun guy, but it just didn't make sense to him that regular everyday citizens had access to firearms that overpower the nation's police force.

So why did police officers have handguns and not rifles? Because, he assumed, they needed something they could quickdraw with one hand, something easy to keep holstered.

They needed their hands free to flip open a tiny notebook and say, "Tell me what happened here."

The latter example was his exact experience as he watched the doors to the ambulance close on either side of Joe, parked in the driveway behind the truck and Anthony's rental car under the night sky.

"I need to go to the hospital, man," he said. "My brother could die while I'm standing here talking to you."

"I'm very sympathetic to that," the officer said unconvincingly. "But you're not goin' anywhere until we get a statement." He was a short man, about forty-five years old, if Anthony had to guess, with a faded military cut that made his hair look like it was growing straight up.

"Tell your buddies to go look at the shed." Anthony pointed. "It's about fifty yards in that direction, and I promise you'll be able to tie the contents to kidnapping, maybe even murder."

"We have a whole team here exploring the premises, sir. Right now, you need to let us do our jobs. You can either give me a statement here, or you can tell me in the back seat of that vehicle over there."

Anthony looked at the police cruiser, the flashing blue and red beams making splotches in his vision. "Will you drive me to the hospital?" It was worth a shot.

The officer considered it for a moment. "Wait here," he said as if Anthony had any time at all to waste.

After taking his sweet time coordinating with the other boys in blue, he came back to Anthony and said, "Get in."

"Got a question for you, Mr. Officer," Anthony said, feeling every second falling off his mental clock. "Do you have any affiliation with the Fellowship of the First Divine?"

The officer's face melted from a bored, glazed look to wide-eyed horror.

"Fuck," he said. "What'd they do this time?"

"Do you?" Anthony asked again.

"Hell no," he said defiantly. "Those lunatics can rot for all I care. Hop in."

Anthony shuffled into the back seat of the cop car, feeling like a badass behind the metal grid. Sure, he wasn't actually arrested, but in his line of work, it was kind of like a badge of honor.

The man in the driver's seat introduced himself as Officer Duffy. "We got about twenty minutes," Duffy said. "Go ahead."

"Where do you want me to start?"

"Wherever you want to."

"All right, but no guarantees you'll believe where this story goes."

A yell ripped through the woods loud enough for Anthony to hear through his side window. "We got fire! We got fire!"

Anthony looked through the haystack of trees, seeing a distant but distinct red and orange accumulation, angry and shapeless, balloon in the direction from which he'd just minutes ago carried Joe's weak body away.

The Fellowship was burning the shed to hide what they'd done.

"Try me," Duffy said.

Three Days Before Deworming

Here were the facts as Anthony Sanderson knew them: The Fellowship of the First Divine was a patriarchal White nationalist cult with the sole purpose of preserving a perfect lineage. The movement's founder, Anders Johanson, believed he was hand-selected by God to carry on the Nordic bloodline. He started the Fellowship of the First Divine in the 1980s, claiming a piece of land within South Point, Virginia, to build a church on top of. As these things go, rumors circulated among the residents of South Point. They said his goal was to create an abundance of offspring before he perished. Originally, the church accrued members organically, but it's not so easy finding people of Nordic descent. So his offspring became his recruiters. New members relocated to join the White Christian utopia, offering a blood sample as part of the application process. Even with a small percentage of Nordic blood, they were admitted.

That was all well and good, but what Anthony truly concerned himself with in relation to the Fellowship was reports of people who had gone missing. From the late 2000s to present, The Fellowship of the First Divine was a known destination for what was colloquially known as conversion therapy. Individuals reportedly came back very different, if they ever came back at all. That's not to mention the handful of men in the greater radius surrounding South Point that had vanished as well.

Anthony Sanderson had a contact on the inside to leverage for his research. Such a shame his brother had seemed too knees-deep in the ideology to be useful until now.

Joe's social media had remained active but with barely any engagement over the past year. The most recent post was from six months ago when he officially tied the knot with a woman named Darla Smithie. From what Anthony could tell, Darla Smithie was an invented identity, though he couldn't uncover who the woman truly was. He only knew that she was a proud member of the Fellowship, and somehow, her fangs had found their way into Anthony's brother.

Joe's status as a rural husband in a White nationalist cult was nothing to Anthony. He'd long been abandoned by his brother. After infiltrating and exposing neo-Nazi groups and far-right militias over the span of five years, the money wasn't coming in like it used to. Journalism was valued less than sensationalism, and so his travel budget had been stripped away. The thing he was good at—embedding himself inside an echo chamber of hate and silently or loudly blending in depending on the scenario—was steadily being replaced with heartless puff pieces retirees would skim through on a Sunday morning in place of a newspaper. It was only a matter of time before the small media agency he worked at was bought out by a huge media conglomerate with no interest in journalism whatsoever.

A story about the Fellowship of the First Divine, with Anthony's inside angle, could propel their agency into the national spotlight, which was exactly how Anthony pitched it to his manager in the corner office of the *Minneapolis Beat*. Kevin, who had stuck his neck out for Anthony several times over, who'd been happy to give him advances when the *Beat* was doing just a tick better than "getting by," appeared more focused on the way the sunlight formed a bright, jagged beam around the Downtown Minneapolis skyline than he was on Anthony's pitch.

"Yo, Kevin," Anthony snapped. "We're talking about the possibility of a streaming deal here. 'Minneapolis Beat presents'... uh ... 'Whities in the Maluland.' I don't know, I'm bad with titles."

"How many people are you going to piss off until you're content with yourself?" Kevin said. "That militia you wrote about eight months ago—"

"The Freedom Keepers?"

"No, the other one."

"Silent Sirens?"

"Whatever. Look, it's a different time now. My family and I don't live in a gated community. We get death threats daily."

"That didn't use to bother you. You said it was just a part of what we do here."

"It's what we *used* to do. I know what you're here to ask me for, and I can't pay you for this. I need you here generating content."

"That doesn't sound like you."

"I can't keep this company running without a huge investment. Maybe someday, we can get things back to how they used to be, but right now, we have to play ball."

"What about the hundreds of people the First Divine have pulled in and brainwashed? Imagine what we could do for them."

"Don't you dare try to placate to my humanitarian side. I know good and well what you do has never been about helping people. You're good at what you do because you have a craving to ruin people."

Anthony crossed his arms, his eyes darting around the room, searching for a defense. "Yeah, but only if they deserve it."

Kevin sat back in his chair. "I'm sorry about your mom, man. Honestly, you shouldn't even be working. I'm not paying for you to travel out to rural Virginia so that you can pretend to be friends with your brother. But we do have a bereavement leave policy. If that's how you choose to spend your time off, so be it."

"I don't have a lot of cash to scrape together for—"

"My hands are tied, man. I'm sorry."

Anthony walked toward the floor-to-ceiling windows, joining Kevin in gazing out at the concrete skyline. "Fine," he said. "I'll get there myself."

Kevin slowly shook his head. "While professionally, I can't condone this, I'll say ... be careful. I know he's your brother, but a group like that ... who knows what kind of skeletons they got buried."

"I intend to dig them up. Without your support, that is." Anthony turned to leave. "Fuck you, Kevin."

"Love you too," Kevin replied. "Don't make this trip personal."

"I never do," Anthony said.

But that was a lie.

Two Days Before Deworming

Anthony rented a compact car for the long drive out of the Richmond airport. Once he drove deep into rural South Point, Virginia, he realized how out of place he would look in the thing. He found himself sharing the road with trucks, bygone models of Oldsmobiles, and John Deere tractors. Strange as it was at this point in his life, the open roads, the fields, and the trees were a nice reprieve from Downtown Minneapolis. Sure, it was more spacious than New York City, but the concrete and steel and glass bored Anthony most days. The people were loud, and anything green was planted in the middle of the sidewalk. South Point reminded Anthony of how he grew up. There were several reasons to hate his upbringing, but summers spent exploring woods, jumping into waist-high creeks, and riding bikes through dirt roads carried a hint of nostalgia that almost made him wish he could return to that time.

The GPS signal went in and out as if struggling to stay awake the closer Anthony got to Joe's house. The neighborhood, as it were, was a small myriad of houses connected to a dirt road, each seemingly surrounded by acres of isolation.

Anthony rumbled down a gravel driveway, the compact car shaking as it inched forward. It must have looked like a tumbleweed in the desert, Anthony thought, but realized it was just a projection of how he himself was feeling in the moment. Two fields on each side with freshly cut grass, healthy trees, and a well led to a ranch-style home with a carport housing one large truck.

This was the property of a retiree. A place that someone would go to to get away after decades of the inherent annoyance that is *other people*. But Joe never seemed to be a guy who needed isolation.

Except from Anthony and their mom, that is.

And then there was Joe, swaying on a rocking chair on the porch facing out to the woods. It was like seeing an alternate version of Joe, though Anthony figured Joe was experiencing the same thing too. Anthony was a floral-print-wearing, thigh-high shorts kind of guy with a quaffed, stylish haircut and tortoise-shell sunglasses, and Joe was a spitting image of rural living. His jeans were faded, not for style but from wear. His eyes were shaded under a hat that probably smelled musty from layers of sweat. Anthony imagined him on a riding lawn mower, beer bottle in hand—no, beer *can*—slowly plowing through acres of grass on a Sunday morning.

Joe sat in the rocking chair staring for longer than Anthony was comfortable with. Maybe he didn't recognize Anthony and was considering running inside to get his shotgun and shoo this outsider away.

Damn, if I'm aiming to stay on his good side, I really have to quit stereotyping, Anthony thought.

"A hug for your long-lost brother?" Anthony called out.

Joe snapped out of it and stood up from the rocking chair. He met Anthony at the bottom of the porch steps and gave him a hug.

"You're not as soft as you used to be," Anthony said. "You been working out?"

"Been haulin' lumber most days for the past year and a half," Joe responded with a slight twang, indicating to Anthony that he'd gone full country.

"You look good," Anthony said, though he didn't really mean it. Some kind of self-sabotage was dragging Joe's skin down under his eyes, whether it was a lack of sleep, drugs, or something else. He and Joe weren't as young as they used to be, and those things didn't have much of a shelf life anymore. They left marks.

"Is your wife home? I'd love to meet her," Anthony said.

"Nah, she's at the church right now. She'll be home later."

"Cool. Then what's on the agenda?"

"I was thinkin' we could go somewhere quiet," Joe said as a grin slid up his cheek. The type of naughty-boy grin Anthony remembered from their teenage years.

"Joe ..."

"Yes, Anthony?"

"I know what that means."

"What's it mean?"

They'd had a long silent gap of years between them, but Anthony couldn't deny that they still had their own special kind of language, an unspoken understanding shared by an unexplainable neural link.

"It means you wanna go shoot some shit," Anthony said.

Joe hid his teeth, trying not to give himself away. "Nah, just go somewhere quiet and talk. Come on."

JOEY POWELL

"I don't do guns, Joe," Anthony said.

Anthony looked to his left at Joe, the truck steering wheel shaking under his open palm. Joe was a bit of an open book regarding his history with Darla. He said that he was in a low place before Darla helped dig him out. For Anthony, the explanation brought to mind a dog rescue video on Instagram, with Joe huddled in a corner, covered in fleas and grime, shaking. The difference was Anthony liked dogs, and he didn't much care for Joe.

Darla had just happened to cross paths with Joe after he moved to Richmond for work. He was enjoying the nightlight "a little too much," as he recalled it. Anthony wondered to what extent little prudish Joe Sanderson could have been enjoying himself.

"I developed a bit of a drinkin' habit," Joe said in a blunt and honest way that made Anthony understand that he had made this admission often. "Honestly, I don't remember a lot of it. I'd show up to work hungover, or I wouldn't show up at all. Just couldn't keep a job. And I was a fool. I ... did a lot of things I'm not proud of. But Darla ... She got me back on track. I've been sober ever since I met her."

"Damn, man. I wish you would have told me," Anthony said. "I would've been there for you." The minute the words left him, Anthony wondered if he actually believed them himself.

They tumbled steadily down a dirt road carved through woods. Eventually, it opened into a junkyard with a cliff lining the dirt about fifty feet from them. Smashed-up cars and broken bottles sat between them and the cliff. Everything had been repurposed as giant punching bags for projectiles, forever in a state of disrepair.

Joe was eager to show Anthony what he was hiding under the cover on the truck bed: a Remington 783 bolt-action rifle, a Mossberg Maverick 88 pistol-grip shotgun, and—Joe's favorite, he said—an AR-15.

As he was prone to do, Anthony inquired as to why Joe needed so many guns, though he already knew what the answer would be. It came out of Joe like a programmed response, prompting Anthony to theorize a scenario in which the buckshot failed to subdue an intruder and the AR-15 was a last resort.

Protection. Anthony had heard the argument often.

He used to go shooting with Joe when they were kids, but he hadn't touched a firearm since he left home to start over. The urge to press Joe on his hobby bulldozed its way to the forefront of Anthony's mind, but he resisted. He wasn't there to argue over Joe's God-given right, a privilege which Anthony seemed to have missed during their Sunday school readings.

Joe handed Anthony protective glasses and earmuffs, as if setting him up for a joke about needing safety equipment just to use the things that presumably kept him safe.

Joe fired a shot from the AR-15, and the bullet nailed the hood of the rusted car ahead of them.

"You're shooting low!" Anthony yelled to hear himself through the earmuffs

"Yeah, no kiddin'!"

The AR was steady, with hardly any recoil at all. Anthony knew it was an incredibly easy gun to shoot, but the bad habit Joe had failed to shake off since he was fifteen meant he'd aim an inch high to compensate, and in doing so, he'd lose the target in the sights.

"Stop staring through the sights and focus on the target!" Anthony yelled. "You always shot better when you trusted your form!"

Anthony's suggestion transformed one of the beer bottles into a satisfying deconstruction of glass shards. He could sense Joe's disappointment at how right he was.

Round after round exploded from the barrel. Shell after shell twirled to the ground. The entire time, Joe didn't bother asking Anthony what he'd been up to the past twelve years.

Anthony had a lie prepared if Joe ever did. One that didn't involve his highly underpaid cult-busting profession.

After a hundred fifty rounds fired, or "two hundred fifty dollars shot," as Joe referred to it, they stopped at a gas station to fill up the truck. That was how Joe thought about shooting, Anthony realized. It was all in terms of dollars and cents. Bullets weren't cheap. Anthony could barely afford his rent on his slim writer's pay, and couldn't tell if he was disgusted or jealous by the brazen waste.

Anthony eyed the car at the pump in front of them—a rusted station wagon covered on the backside with an assortment of bumper stickers. One logo in particular, containing a globe with all the continents colored with rainbow stripes, caught his eye. He knew it to be a symbol of the Pluralist Society, a controversial progressive group. He wondered what the hell they were doing out here in an area where

Anthony would bet good money the residents wanted to bring back sundown towns.

As Joe went through the steps of getting the gas pump operational, Anthony glanced at the double doors of the gas station, wondering if fate would rear its head and put a PluSoc supporter in close vicinity to his cult follower brother.

He didn't have to wait long.

A tall guy in a beanie and a long baggy t-shirt left the checkout counter and headed toward the station wagon. He must have been in his early twenties—one of those idealistic fresh-out-of-college types—with light-brown skin and patchy black facial hair. How the guy wasn't sweating his balls off under the beanie, Anthony couldn't understand.

Anthony could hear the forthcoming conversation playing out. One in which Joe instructed him to fear PluSoc, a group that preached inclusively but bred division. A group running astroturfed campaigns to indoctrinate children and turn them away from the truth. A group that assaulted police officers and launched false flag operations as effortlessly as children playing in a sandbox.

A bunch of dumb lies only dumb people believed.

As Anthony sat in the passenger's seat, all he could do was hope Joe didn't see the bumper sticker and would let this guy go about his day. Undeniably, though, a piece of him wondered how a confrontation would play out. He wondered whether Virginia had a castle doctrine. Maybe Joe would flop to the ground like a soccer player, reach for a concealed weapon, and fire, only to say later that he feared for his life.

JOEY POWELL

The guy in the beanie opened his driver's side door, but before he could get into his car, Joe asked him, "You handin' out flyers tryin' to recruit people for your incredible cause?"

And that was the answer to Anthony's question. Joe had seen the bumper sticker.

The guy thought about it for a second, then closed the door with the creak of a rusty hinge. "What?"

"You think I don't know what you are?"

The guy stared at Joe and gave a shrug.

"Joe," Anthony called out through the car window, "knock it off."

"The bumper sticker on your car," Joe said, ignoring Anthony.

The guy moved closer to look at the back of his own car, closing the space between him and Joe. "Got a lot of bumper stickers. Could you be more specific?"

"Tell me," Joe said. "Was it you who bombed that abortion clinic about fifty miles away, or was it one of your buddies? We don't take kindly to acts of terrorism around here, especially when they're used as a false flag."

Anthony knew Joe expected to get a harsh reaction—some outburst of emotion—but all the guy did was laugh, his eyebrows rising into the fibers of his beanie. He laughed at Joe the way people laugh at a joke that doesn't land, a joke too stupid to be genuinely funny.

The guy gave the front of Joe's truck a light pat, causing Joe to flinch.

The gas pump clicked, signaling to Joe that his truck was full. He reached down to remove the pump from his vehicle as the guy drove away.

SQUIRMING ALL THE WAY UP

When he got back in the car, he asked Anthony if he thought the kid was Mexican, Puerto Rican, or something else. For some reason, the ambiguity of his light-brown skin bothered Joe.

It bothered him a great deal.

"Come on inside," Joe said. "I want you to meet my wife."

Stepping out of the car was a major reprieve from the exhausting and mind-numbing conversation Anthony had had with Joe on the ride back. He already knew the story and was intimately familiar with either side's reporting on it.

Bart Shaw, host of the podcast TrutherWire, put out an open call for listeners to write in if they knew of any clinics performing abortions in their state. He collected the names of clinics and then went to great lengths to find the home addresses of the doctors he believed were performing the abortions. It instantly put their lives in danger, and for some reason, good Christian Joe thought that was completely fine.

One listener, however, claimed to know of an abortion clinic that was also performing gender-affirming care. The logistics of that didn't make sense, as a hospital would need completely different personnel, but that didn't stop Bart Shaw from spreading the rumor. That's the thing about lies—you can tell yourself you're not a liar if the lie you're telling came from someone else.

A bomb was planted in that clinic, which just so happened to be in Virginia. After the threat was called in, a bomb squad showed up and deemed the explosive to be faulty.

JOEY POWELL

Everyone blamed Shaw for what could have been absolute carnage, but Shaw stated that no God-fearing person would ever perpetrate such hate. He told his listeners that the bomb must have been planted by PluSoc agitators who wanted him and his audience behind bars.

Why would a progressive group plant a bomb in a hospital just to cancel a guy who runs a podcast? It wasn't Anthony's job to understand the rationale, only to report on the paranoia, the alternate-reality denialism of a group that would believe the words of a demagogue and accuse others of gullibility.

See, Joe didn't pretend to understand what went on in the mind of a progressive. If they'll believe anything, he imagined they'd *do* just about anything to promote their agenda.

Anthony had listened for what seemed like hours but had only spanned fifteen minutes. He didn't bother to mention that the bomb was a dud and therefore couldn't have been planted by a progressive. Progressives aren't dumb.

The bomb would have gone off.

Darla was in the kitchen when they came in, stirring mashed potatoes and wafting a smooth buttery smell with each revolution. Peering over her shoulder, she gave Anthony a smile so strained it would have looked more natural had she sketched it in crayon, like the muscles in her cheeks were fighting back. Anthony gave her a big smile in return.

"Darla!" Anthony exclaimed, spreading his arms wide.

She turned away from the stove and offered him a hand. Anthony wasn't sure what he expected from the woman who made his brother an honest cult follower, but the thought of the stereotypical rural folk being warm and welcoming had crossed his mind. That wasn't quite the experience he was getting.

"Not a hugger, I see," Anthony said.

"It's nice to meet you, Anthony. I've heard so much about you." After a few jerks up and down, she broke free of his hand. Firm grip for a small woman.

"And I know so very little about you," Anthony said, "but we're going to change that. Thank you so much for welcoming me into your home. This was unexpected but quite the pleasant surprise."

"We're happy to have you," Darla said, though she didn't look it. "I'm sorry about the passing of your mother. Truly. God rest her soul."

"Oh, thank you for saying that."

"If there's anything we can do to make your stay more comfortable, please—"

"Come on, Darla, I'm not checking into a Ritz Carlton here. I'm sure the amenities are perfect for my very low-maintenance needs. I got by on Ramen noodles for years. Give me a mattress, a bedsheet, and a book, and I'm living in luxury."

Darla wasn't sure how to take that. "Good to know. I'm sure you'll find our meals slightly better than ... Ramen." She walked back to the stove. "You boys wash up. Dinner'll be done in ten. Anthony, I left a towel and a washcloth in the guest bathroom for you."

"Aren't you the sweetest?" Anthony said.

"She sure is." Joe gave Darla a kiss on the cheek, and she giggled performatively. They seemed like a perfectly loving couple. "I'm gonna go wash up. Let you two get acquainted."

With Joe gone, Anthony leaned over the kitchen counter, flashing a smile in Darla's periphery.

"What did y'all get up to today?" Darla asked, trying and failing to sound pleasant.

"Shot some guns," Anthony told her. "Well ... more specifically, Joe shot some guns and I watched."

"Makes sense that a boy like you doesn't like shootin'."

"That obvious, huh?" Anthony chuckled. "I want to say thanks for having me here. I know it probably feels like Joe sprung me on you, but you've been very welcoming, and I appreciate that."

"My pleasure." She forced the words through her teeth like a slab of beef through a meat grinder.

"So it's been about six months together, right? Would've thought you'd have about five kids by now. Joe always talked about having a big—"

"We haven't been able to conceive."

"Oh, I ... I didn't mean to—"

"Of course you didn't."

"It's really none of my business, Darla. I'm sorry."

"You're right. It's not."

Anthony stood up straight and rounded the counter to occupy a more prominent spot in Darla's field of vision. "You know ... my boyfriend and I have been discussing alternative methods like surrogacy or adoption. If you need some information, I'm happy to—"

"I didn't say we *can't*." Darla met his eyes with an angry, unwelcoming expression. "I said we haven't been able to. It's just God's plan for us now. When he sees fit to bless us with a child, he will."

"Don't you think you should consult with a specialist just to make—"

"We don't need a specialist."

Regardless of his purpose in that house, Anthony couldn't help but feel sorry for Darla and Joe, assuming their sex had become passionless, hopeful of a gift that may never come. Maybe. Darla didn't realize there are some things faith couldn't redirect, and that sometimes humans are at the whims of their own biology.

Anthony had noticed the Nordic runes displayed prominently in the living room when he first entered the house. Given Darla's history with the church, it made sense to Anthony that she would hang them like small shrines everywhere with such emphatic pride.

"Are those Nordic symbols?" Anthony asked, feigning ignorance as he took his place at the small kitchen table.

"Runes, yes," Darla replied.

"Did you know we have a Nordic strain?" Joe asked Anthony. "Small percentage of our heritage, but it's there."

"Never really bothered to look," Anthony said. "That makes up a pretty small percentage of Americans, right? Did you two meet each other at a Vikings cosplay meet-up?"

Darla and Joe gave him blank looks in return. Apparently, cosplay hadn't made its way to rural Virginia.

"I'm very proud of my heritage, Anthony," Darla said. "You should be as well."

The way Anthony saw it, he didn't choose his heritage; therefore, he never saw value in celebrating it.

His eyes landed on the portrait on the living room wall of an overweight white man with white hair and a white mustache wearing a white suit, looking like Colonel Sanders.

"Who's the esteemed gentleman on the wall over there?" Anthony asked, though he already knew.

Darla smiled. "That's the founder of the Fellowship of the First Divine. Anders Johanson. He's a great man. *Was*, anyway."

"Is that a church? How long have you been with the ... Fellowship, is it?" He was laying it on thick, but Darla was none the wiser.

"A while," she said blandly.

They all went quiet. Sometime between the scrape of utensils against their plates and the wet mashing of food in their mouths, Darla snuck a glance at Joe—a glance that Anthony caught as well.

"I'd like for us to sit down tonight and uh ..." Joe fidgeted in his seat. "I'd like for us to do some Bible study."

"Okay," Anthony said apathetically. "Did you have a passage in mind?"

"Yeah, I got a few."

"We know you may have a different ... perspective," Darla said, "But all perspectives are welcome."

"Say what?" Anthony responded.

"Honey ..." Joe said, trying to call her off.

"No, I'm curious to know what she meant by my 'perspective'," Anthony said. "That thing which is apparently very welcome here."

"Anthony, I'm fully aware of your sexual orientation, and I mean you no offense," Darla said. "You're very welcome here."

"You don't have to act offended," Joe said. "I accept you. I always have."

"Oh, you *always* have?" Anthony replied.

"Just because I don't agree with homosexuality, it doesn't mean I can't have love in my heart for you."

"Whom I love is not an *opinion* for you to *disagree* with. And it's not like bad food that doesn't *agree* with your stomach."

Darla cut in: "What is it then?"

"Darla," Anthony said, "can you pump the breaks a bit?"

"Don't talk to her like that," Joe said.

Things were flying off the rails fast, but Anthony needed to add a little more track before the train was gone for good. "Okay, Joe. Why don't you ... 'agree' with it?"

All of sudden, he felt like he had stacked ten years of distance in the form of bricks piled on top of Joe's chest. His brother's eyes were locked on the woodgrain of the table, refusing to look in Anthony's direction.

"We never talked about it," Anthony said. "So tell me."

Joe said, quite delicately, "It's impossible for two men to reproduce. It's unnatural. That's all."

Anthony looked back and forth between Darla and Joe. He knew what he was about to say would light a match and launch it onto the river of gasoline that was the silence between the three of them. But he felt that it had to be said.

"But ... You two can't conceive ..." Anthony said it in such a matter-of-fact way, making Joe's logic exchange hands.

After a tense moment, Darla dropped her silverware on her plate, making sure the contact was sharp and dramatic. She rose quickly from her seat, the legs scraping against the cheap vinyl floor, and stormed out.

"Why'd you have to do that?" Joe asked Anthony.

"It wasn't an insult."

"It was taken as one."

Anthony tilted his head and let out a small laugh, quiet enough for Darla not to hear.

"Why is this funny to you?" Joe asked.

"What do you wanna do here, bud? Be honest with me."

"First, I'm gonna have to ask you to apologize to my wife."

"Yeah, sure. I'll apologize as soon as we're finished talking. But you have to tell me what the hell I'm doing here."

Joe struck a serious tone, his eyes landing on the table again. "Mom's death hit me hard."

"Yeah, I know it did. It hit me hard too."

"I can't stand the idea of not seeing Mom again," he said.

"Oh ..." A lightbulb went off in Anthony's head. "You think she's in Hell, and now you're afraid I'll be there too ... Because I'm—"

"Homosexuality has nothing to do with it," Joe said. "God forgives sin. I just can't let you leave here without accepting the word of God."

Anthony had his angle. He hadn't been invited to make up for lost time; he'd been invited for a soft conversion. He'd been invited to learn the—capital T—"Truth" because poor, confused, college-educated Anthony wasn't capable of deciphering truth from lies.

It took a while for Darla to answer the door of the owner's bedroom, long enough that Anthony announced to her that he wanted to apologize just to get her attention.

Darla never responded verbally, though Anthony could hear rustling from the other side of the door. When it finally opened, Darla's black hair was offset, the middle part twisted unnaturally away from the center of her forehead. A streak of blood curled under her chin, forming a droplet around the neckline of her blouse. She seemed not to notice. Her smile was euphoric, displaying the gaps between her back teeth and cheeks. Her eyes were wider than Anthony had seen them, revealing red hooks around the edges of her eyeballs.

"All is forgiven," she said, then shut the door.

Anthony knew she was wearing a wig. And though he'd seen people bleed, he'd never seen someone so happy to be bleeding.

The sun hung like a lip over the trees when Anthony joined Joe on the porch. They swayed on the rocking chairs, talking about everything and nothing at the same time like they used to. Joe had given up on Bible study for the time being.

Later that night, Anthony was awoken by footsteps and found his brother sleepwalking. He called out to Joe, but Joe was unresponsive. A red tear of blood hung down under a red circle that appeared to be a hickey from a shark bite.

Between that and the blood drooling from Darla's wig, Anthony knew something very strange was going on in the house. Whatever Joe was into, he was probably beyond saving, but it was something Anthony had made peace with since before he'd even arrived. Frankly, he felt that Joe didn't deserve any intervention. It was an idea Anthony came back to often in his work. When people are led to believe and do terrible things, do we blame the leader or the followers? People have free will, don't they?

People choose to accept what they let inside.

JOEY POWELL

Twelve Hours Before Deworming

Darla wasn't around that morning, though she'd left her mark with the smell of bacon, eggs, and biscuits. Joe seemed prepared for Anthony's arrival at the table, jumping to attention and scrambling feverishly to make a plate.

Anthony told Joe he saw him sleepwalking the night before and watched as his face went flush. "Bad dream?" Anthony said.

"Somethin' like that," Joe replied. He explained that he had just started sleepwalking that week. As for the gash on his shoulder, he had no explanation. Joe seemed content bleeding from his arm each night.

That Anthony forgot to say grace before eating was a slip-up and momentarily turned any pleasantry sideways. Joe led the prayer, and they ate.

Anthony turned the key in the ignition of his small rental car, failing to turn the engine over. He watched as an unmistakable look of relief washed over Joe's face, who obviously wouldn't want his fellow townsfolk to see him in Anthony's compact vehicle

"Nope, can't get it to start," Anthony said. "And here I was thinking I'd do the driving today."

SQUIRMING ALL THE WAY UP

"It's gotta be the battery," Joe said. "I'm surprised the rental company gave it to you dead like this. I can get someone out to tow it."

"I'm not paying for it, man. I'll just call the rental company and have someone fix it before I leave."

"You sure? I could get an auto shop to just pop in a new battery for ya."

Anthony was already out of the car, pulling up the contact information for the rental company.

"How's the reception out here?" he asked Joe.

"Spotty in most places. Decent if you stand still."

"Then I'll take a walk and find a spot. I need to burn off that breakfast."

"Just ... by yourself?"

"Yeah. I'll come back in ten minutes tops."

"All right, then. Don't get lost." Joe walked back up the porch stairs and into the house.

Anthony stood outside soaking in the silence, hearing his own breathing, without a car horn or the screech of tires to interrupt the peaceful melody.

He walked down the driveway and onto the dirt road, thinking he'd go about a quarter of a mile down and back just to stretch his legs. Joe had been right in his warning—Anthony's phone couldn't hold a signal long enough to make a call.

A few long steps from the mouth of the driveway, Anthony decided to take Joe's advice and stand in place. He tapped the call button again.

A soft scream echoed through the woods.

It was so alien amongst the hum of the breeze, the bugs, the birds, like a radio signal intercepted for a split second.

He turned back toward Joe's property, his eyeline cutting through the woods in the direction of the sound.

Anthony Sanderson was an investigative journalist. So he investigated.

It was difficult for Anthony to remain incognito over the leaves and twigs piled high on every inch of the woodland ground. Beyond giving himself away, he didn't want to miss another scream because of the thin crunches under his feet.

He froze, realizing he wasn't the only one in the woods. A second set of feet sent snapping *clacks* into the air like lettuce being ripped.

Anthony found cover, angling away from the direction of the footsteps.

A large elderly man, balding with a ring of white hair, walked into view wearing a cassock shirt tucked into jeans. The pastor walked through the woods and toward the dirt road, oblivious to Anthony's presence.

Once enough distance was between them, Anthony moved forward in the direction the old man had come.

He came across a small wooden shed in a flat clearing surrounded by trees. Fixed at the center of the shed was a latched door, with windows on either side and warped wood strips coated in moss. An odd spot for a shed, Anthony thought, as it was a long distance from the house.

As he went closer to the shed, Anthony realized the latch was free. An open padlock had been left hanging from it.

Anthony took quiet steps ...

Reached out for the latch ...

But the door opened before he could reach it.

The sudden realization that he'd been discovered sent a chill bursting through his spine.

"Anthony?" Darla stood in the door frame. She looked confused at first, then smiled. "What are you doing out here?"

"Sorry, I was ... taking a walk and thought I heard a scream. Did you hear it?"

"A scream? Heavens, no." She wore a vacant expression to juxtapose her 1950s Hollywood starlet delivery.

"And there was a man—an older guy—walking through the woods."

"There was?"

"Yeah. Big guy, white hair. He was wearing one of those, ya know ..." He pointed to his collarbone. "Priest collar things."

"Oh, of course. That was Father Henry. Did he frighten you?"

"No, I just ... thought you'd want to know about a guy on your property is all."

Anthony looked around her shoulder, peering into the shed.

"We keep the lawn and gardening equipment in there. Pastor Henry was helping me with my work."

"You keep your tools this far from the house?"

"It's a lot of land to cover."

"And it's all yours, huh?"

"It's *ours*, yes."

"You know, I'd like to sit down with you sometime and talk about how you managed to snag this property. Jared and I have been talking about moving out of the city soon and starting a family."

"Well, I certainly wish you the best with that."

Ice ... Cold ...

Darla closed the shed door behind her and fixed the lock on the latch, killing any shot Anthony had at seeing what was in there.

"Could I walk you back to the house?" she asked.

"Absolutely. I could regale you with stories from Joe's childhood."

"Wouldn't that be fun?"

"Oh, you have no idea."

Anthony prided himself on his ability to bullshit. After the several stank-faced looks and the hokie chuckles from Darla, he made it his primary mission to get a laugh out of her. If he could get her to open up just a little bit, maybe he could figure out what made Joe Sanderson such an easy mark to dig her claws into.

It didn't work, and the walk was rather miserable.

Anthony knew he'd heard a scream and knew where it had come from, and all the angels and demons on Earth wouldn't stop him from getting into that shed. In due time.

CHAPTER THREE

Fifty-Nine Minutes After Deworming

Joe remembered his life before Darla as a series of sexual encounters with women whose faces he couldn't remember. Most nights had a similar cadence. A stroll through Downtown led to a shot at a bar led to another shot with a woman led to a dance led to him falling onto a mattress with a stranger. Then he'd leave the next morning. Over and over and over again like a clock going forward and backward, playing through his woozy head as he slipped in and out of consciousness.

He remembered not being able to keep a job. He would show up drunk or not show up at all. He tried Alcoholics Anonymous, but it couldn't keep him out of the liquor cabinet.

My name's Joe, and I'm an alcoholic.

Hi, Joe.

He remembered one day when he was feeling particularly rough and probably looked it too, he heard a sweet voice calling to him as he walked out of the ABC Store. That was when he saw Darla for the first time, wearing a cute sun dress spotted with daisies. She nervously asked if he could help her with her car, which was immobile at the gas station on the opposite side of the road. He hesitated at first, unsure why such a beautiful young woman wanted help from a man with a paper bag full of cheap whiskey.

He never did make it into that bag.

Joe couldn't recall how much time had passed between then and his official commitment to his sobriety, but he did remember Darla cradling his head as he lay on the ground, dripping sweat, shaking, and crying.

His stomach had felt queasy the whole time he was going through withdrawals, but he never threw up. It felt like a bad stomach bug, but worse. Everything inside his gut was squirming like pinwheels in his intestines.

Joe realized as he looked up at the fluorescent lights of the ambulance interior, needles poking at him, hands grabbing at him, that Darla had used his sickness to infect him with the worms.

She'd masked the sickness of the goddamn worms with the sickness of withdrawals.

Six Hours Before Deworming

"He's out there waitin' for you," Darla said behind him, causing him to jump and inadvertently end the call on the landline phone.

"Dang, you scared me," he said, touching his chest. "I thought you was at the church."

Darla smiled and fluttered her eyelids in a cutesy way. "Nope, had to tend to some work here."

"Ah. Anthony's car won't start, so I was callin' some mechanics to see if they can help him out. He says the rental company'll fix it, but I'd like to see if we can do him a solid." Joe noticed the smile hadn't left Darla's face and her eyes weren't matching her lips. It morphed into a crazed look that Joe didn't understand, so he just kept talking. "We're gonn' to play some basketball. Just like old t—"

"You remember why you brought him here, right?" Darla asked Joe in a hushed tone.

"Uh ... yeah. I brought him here to reconnect. And maybe encourage him to follow the right path."

"People like that don't need encouragement, Joe."

"Darla—"

"I talked to Father Castor. I know your purpose. Not sure why you chose to not tell me, but that's fine."

Yeah, of course Father Castor went and blabbed to my wife, Joe thought, considering never confiding in the kid again. "I didn't mean to—"

"It's between you and God, honey. I just feel the need to remind you that your brother is corrupt, and as long as he believes he can live in sin, he'll be bound to Hell. Is the purpose of the Fellowship not to save the irredeemable?"

Save him, the voice inside of Joe said. *Don't let him infect you like he did your mother.*

Joe walked outside and told Anthony they needed to make one quick stop before going out to the blacktop. Anthony pumped up an old, balding basketball in the passenger's seat as Joe veered off the dirt road and out of the neighborhood. Once they were on a paved street, Anthony finally had a good signal.

Anthony didn't call the rental company, though. He called his boyfriend. Joe didn't listen too closely to the conversation, but did hear Anthony say, "I love you."

Joe tried to recount the last time he had said those words to Darla and she last said them back.

He couldn't think of anything recent.

Five Hours Before Deworming

Joe knew Anthony didn't have a good relationship with church and half expected him to sprint in the opposite direction like a vampire at sun-up. To his brother's credit, though, he kept it cool. He walked straight with Joe and took a seat at a pew.

Joe didn't realize this was something he missed—sitting in a pew next to the brother he used to have. It was an experience he found himself desiring to have again and again, imagining Anthony on one side, Darla on the other. He and he alone had the power to make that happen. God had deemed it so.

"I want to tell you a story of God's grace," Joe said, settling into the hard cushion of the pew, his spine stabbing the wood at his back. "So that you can see His true power." He looked around the church, practically able to hear his own breath echo between the walls. Not a soul around save for the two of them.

With Anthony his audience of one, the words didn't so much come out of Joe's mouth as they did pour out of him. He described himself as being at a low point in his life before he met Darla. He'd been doing shots with a cute brunette at a bar. She looked young. A dancer-type, he said. Thin but toned. And since she had very little body fat, she got drunk pretty quickly. He met a lot of women on a lot of nights, but this brunette was something special. What was her name? It started with a B—Blakely? Beverly? He described them falling into bed together, detailing their limbs wrapping around each other in drunken passion almost in a reminiscent way. Joe said he knew what he was doing was wrong, but in the moment, he didn't care. He was having fun, just like every other drunken lay before her. The unavoidable black hole occupied his chest the next morning every time, knowing that there was nothing to attach his heart to, that such sensation could end in total anonymity, was just a casualty of the act.

Anthony interrupted. "It's just sex, Joe."

But it wasn't *just sex*. It was *sin*. "Please just let me get through this," Joe said.

Joe got a call one day. It was the brunette with the body of a dancer. One woman out of so many women on so many nights. She told him she was pregnant. His entire world froze. He'd screwed up, and he had to think quickly.

The ride to the clinic was quiet and shattered every nerve in his being. This woman, whose name he did not know, could have asked him to turn around at any moment. He wasn't ready to have a child. He had told himself God didn't desire this for him now. So he drove her there and helped her check in. As they were waiting in the lobby, Joe said he needed to get something from his car.

But he got in his car and left.

She tried calling, but he didn't pick up. He cried all the way to his apartment and cried into his pillow the rest of the night, finally falling asleep in a waterfall of booze.

Joe was rambling so much and his brain was so tangled with agonizing memories that he couldn't tell what he was and wasn't articulating, but he heard himself say, "That woman committed the most egregious sin imaginable, and I have to live with knowing that I told her to do it, that *I* drove her there." He couldn't face Anthony. He feared how his brother would react to the wrong he'd done. When tears spouted from Joe's eyes, he thought it might've been easier to face his brother since the tears blurred everything in a fat, wet cloud. "All children are born into sin, Anthony. And because of me, that child never had a chance at Heaven. That child is in Hell for an eternity because of me. It was such a weight on my shoulders that I couldn't keep it from Darla. I had to let her know my indefensible sin. The first question she asked was, 'Have you repented?' I said I had. And she said, 'Then God has forgiven you.' That was all I needed to hear. The Fellowship has changed me. I'm a better man because of it, and now I have the opportunity to correct my misdeeds. That's why I asked you to come here."

One of Joe's trembling hands found his eyes and wiped them as he finally looked at Anthony.

"You selfish little narcissist," Anthony said. "You mourn for the embryo but won't ask forgiveness for leaving that woman in the dark?" He stood. "And then say *she* committed an egregious sin?" Anthony blew a heated breath out of his chest, a burst of spit shotgunning from his mouth. "Fuck you, man. I'm gonna go explore the town. Stay here and have a pity party with someone who gives a shit. I don't have to listen to this anymore."

Anthony fled the church, making soft stomps against the red liner separating two columns of pews, leaving Joe to silently wallow in his sadness. Where would he go?

Joe didn't have the energy to run after him. He lowered his head and listened to the footsteps get more distant.

The double doors sent a clap through the door when they closed.

"Let him go, son," a squeaky voice called out to Joe near the church stage.

Joe looked up to see Father Castor, bright-eyed as ever. He wasn't in the mood for the pastor-in-training and ineffectually replied, "Hello, Father. Didn't realize you were here. I thought you'd be at home."

"This is my home, son." Father walked closer to Joe, seeming to hover underneath the edges of his robe. "I'm very sorry that conversation went the way it did. I'm afraid your brother is as lost as Darla described."

Joe's face twisted in confusion.

"It's a small community, son," Father Castor said. "People talk." He smiled. "Could you give me a hand downstairs?"

"Uh, all right," Joe said, giving his eyes another rub. Truthfully, he wasn't in any position to do anything.

"Come with me," Father Castor said.

Joe followed him down the red carpet and past the stage. "You must be very excited to have your brother here," he said with his back turned to Joe.

"Sure," Joe said, his nose still raw from wiping it. He followed the young pastor through the back door.

"Close that door behind you," Father Castor said.

Joe did as he asked.

They descended a flight of stairs into the basement area, which housed tables and chairs and had been used primarily for Bible studies and event planning, a place more intimate than the main area.

Across the checkered-tile floor in the corner of the room was a wooden door with a bulky old lock above the handle.

Father Castor pointed to the door. "Do you know where that leads?" he asked.

"I was told it's an old tunnel that was sealed up decades ago," Joe answered.

Father Castor let out an uncomfortable sigh, appearing disappointed. "There should be no secrets in a marriage, Joe. God did not create the institution so that men and women could deceive each other. I believe in due time, Darla would have been forthcoming about your true purpose, but ... well, I think you need to see for yourself what's really at stake here."

"I'm ... not sure I understand, Father."

"That conversation you just had with your brother, the homosexual. I don't want him corrupting your faith."

"My faith is not corruptible, Father—"

"As long as the Devil walks among us, everyone's faith is corruptible." The pastor struck a dead serious tone, his boyish face appearing to age twenty years in weathered anger. He put a hand in the pocket of his long robe and took out a small set of keys, thumbing through them until he found the right one.

"This is what she should have shown you the day y'all shared your vows."

Joe expected to see nothing behind the door—a collection of rocks clustered and crushed within the frame. Instead, a dark set of stone steps descended before him, the light of the basement making only the first few steps visible. The remaining steps vanished into a black hole of darkness. A metal fixture hung against the wall with a torch placed through it. Father Castor removed a lighter from his robe and lit the torch, casting a bright radius of light.

"Close that door behind you," Father Castor said again.

As Joe walked down the stone steps, he began to feel like he was leaving the natural world and entering some sort of Hell.

"There's no need to be afraid," Father Castor said.

But Joe wasn't so sure.

Further and further down they went until the air behind Joe's eardrums compressed.

The stairwell led to a stone surface, appearing underneath the torchlight with centuries of wear.

Father Castor stopped and turned to Joe, the torch lighting his profile while his other half remained shrouded in darkness. "I understand you didn't *choose* the All-Father," he said. "Darla has chosen to deploy the All-Father when you dream. I believe she thought you'd be afraid. The All-Father craves followers, and frankly, I feel her own personal needs have clouded her judgment. But it's clear that the All-Father has chosen to speak to you, and that, son ... is a true blessing. He doesn't speak to everyone."

He lowered the torch, bringing into view a stone basin that appeared like a fountain. The flame caught the liquid within the basin and sprinted wider, forming a half-circle and lighting the space around them. It was then, encased in the horseshoe of fire, that Joe realized they were in a cavernous pocket far below the surface of the world, with stalactites hanging down like teeth high above them.

The space around the edges of the flame was black and deep, but Joe had a terrible, unavoidable feeling that something was down there, something his eyes failed to recognize.

Something slithering around the column upon which they stood.

"What ... is this?" he asked Father Castor through quickened breaths.

"It's everything you haven't been shown. I'm lifting the veil so that you can understand what needs to be done. What do you think that mark on your shoulder came from?"

Joe raised his sleeve, revealing the purple outline above his bicep. "I don't know."

Father Castor separated the sides of his robe and pulled up his undershirt, revealing an identical purple outline around his belly. "It's how the All-Father speaks to us," he said.

"What is the All-Father?" Joe asked.

Then the hissing came.

"The All-Father and I have a special connection. I know what He needs. I know what this congregation needs. Since He speaks to you, I think He believes you can help us get there." The hissing got louder. "Ya see, Darla and Henry think that they can serve Him just by hosting a few of his offspring. I realized recently that if I continue to consume the offspring, my connection to Him grows stronger."

The hissing became unbearably loud. Joe pressed his palms against his ears.

SQUIRMING ALL THE WAY UP

Father Castor yelled over the noise. "I also realized that I can share my vision with you! Come closer!"

Joe stepped forward. "What is that sound?!"

"I'm going to put my hand on your forehead!" Father Castor yelled. "Be very quiet now! I need to concentrate!"

He closed his eyes and held a warm palm against Joe's forehead. The hissing continued, sounding like a mix between a snake pit and a swarm of bees, all circling Joe's head and shaking his brain.

Joe scanned the surrounding area with his eyes, curious as to what all of this was leading to.

A slimy figure rose from the deep pit behind the fire, something slick and fat and writhing. Its insides scrunched under thin translucent skin, containing what Joe's mind could only interpret as a universe. Stars and planets and rings and floating rocks, reds and blues and golds against an endless black void, all dancing in the jumbled mess of a wild, boneless appendage.

"Dear God," Joe said.

"Stay still," Father Castor said. "Trust in me, son."

A mouth opened at the end of it, the skin peeling back to reveal a circle of small teeth. It appeared to sway excitedly in the air as it made its way toward Father Castor, the teeth gliding inches away from Joe's sweating nose, eventually sliding under Castor's robe and forming a bulge in his stomach.

The creature formed a twisting line like a roller coaster track, running from Father Castor's belly, twisting over the fire, and vanishing into the depths of the surrounding area that the circle of fire couldn't reach.

JOEY POWELL

A vibrating sensation tickled Joe's skull, like a hundred fingers exploring the grooves of his brain. He looked at Father Castor as nodules in the young man's forehead swam like tadpoles along his skin.

The young pastor tilted his head and gasped. "See."

Then Castor's vision poured into Joe's consciousness until he was no longer surrounded by physical space. The vile voice in his head grew louder as images of a world in ruin flashed in quick succession.

A city in flames. *They'll burn everything if we let them!*

Buildings crumbling in a tidal wave of debris. *They'll destroy our infrastructure until there's nothing left!*

Faceless people with dark skin color smashing windows, launching bombs at uniformed police officers. *Our cities will be in ashes, and it will be our fault for letting it happen!*

A somber, starved group of Whites—hundreds, if not thousands—stood behind a tall fence, banished to internment camps. *They seek to replace us!*

Nursery beds devoid of children.

The vision went black, and Joe fell to the ground.

Castor stumbled with him but kept his footing. The slimy arm whipped back into the depths of the pit.

"You see now," Castor said. "The All-Father told you to save your brother, but he's one piece of a much, much larger puzzle. The All-Father needs us to save ourselves."

Joe should have been frightened by what he'd seen. An otherworldly being of unknown origin projecting images into his mind.

But he wasn't afraid. The tears he had left to cry were tears of joy, for he had seen the image of God from his dreams.

"God is real," Joe sobbed.

"And He is mighty," Father Castor responded, his face curling into a smile.

CHAPTER FOUR

Five Hours Before Deworming

Anthony wanted to tell Joe it was just sex. He wanted Joe to know that purity culture had altered his brain chemistry to think that sex was a joyless act in service of conception, that he shouldn't be ashamed, but it was pointless. All he could think about now was this nameless woman sitting in a lobby, waiting for the return of a man who didn't care about her, not knowing that she would go on to exist as a nameless entity on his lips.

He waited by the truck for ten minutes before Joe came out of the church. Between the diner and the laundromat, there wasn't much to explore on foot, and he'd be damned if he got lost in a quiet town where people reportedly went missing.

He expected to see Joe distraught and conflicted, but the Joe presented before him had his eyes spread wide, unnaturally so, looking like he'd seen an anomaly. The expression wasn't joy or sadness but rather amazement.

The distance between them shortened quickly. Joe put a hand on Anthony's shoulder and said, "I'm so very glad you're here with me, brother." He walked past Anthony and cranked open the driver's side door.

Anthony had expected some kind of self-reflection spurred by his vitriolic reaction to Joe's story, but Joe appeared like a simple, enlightened man who just unlocked something previously unknowable. His face carried that religious glaze of wondrous belief that Anthony was all too familiar with.

"Let's go have some fun," Joe hollered over the top of his half-lowered window.

"But we're really going to the court, right?" Anthony asked.

"Yep, no more pit stops." Joe grinned.

Once the truck was in motion, Anthony decided to press Joe a bit harder.

"So I was talking to one of the locals, and she told me there's an application process to get accepted into the Fellowship. That true?"

"Someone just randomly said that to you?" Joe asked.

It wasn't a subtle segue. Maybe Anthony was losing his touch, he thought. He gave a confident, "Yeah," which seemed to work fine on Joe.

"Why are you askin'?" Joe said.

"I've just never heard of a church making people apply."

"Yeah, I did the application process. It's not what it sounds like."

"What do *you* think it sounds like?"

"They just want to make sure they're only acceptin' true believers. I don't know what you've heard or read—"

"I haven't heard or read anything," Anthony lied.

Joe smiled, his mood having completely shifted since he left the church. But Anthony could fix that. Getting a rise out of Joe was the most fun he'd had the entire trip.

"I'm well aware of how the 'media' portrays us." Joe emphasized the word "media" with finger quotes as if the concept of media wasn't real. "None of it is true."

"But why is it important that you get a blood test to join the church? Are only people with certain types of heritage admitted?"

Joe's face dropped. "Again, I'm not sure what you've heard, but I don't concern myself with rumors. You'd be wise to shut your mouth about it. These are my people you're talkin' about. We're doing important work."

Anthony felt Joe tensing up, mobilizing his defenses. It was a perfect opportunity to push his buttons and see what other kinds of admissions he would make.

"Would I be admitted?"

Joe didn't respond.

"I wouldn't be, right? Because of my filthy little habit?"

"Because you're a perversion of God's plan," Joe said.

"Whoa, we're just coming out and saying it, huh?"

"I'm tryin' to help you."

"Yeah, okay."

"How dare you mock—"

"No, how dare you?!" Anthony's voice slapped the casing of the metal cage they rode in. "You texted me the night Mom died, and you haven't asked about her once. How stupid of me to think you might've felt the least bit regretful for cutting us out of your life for an entire decade. A *decade,* Joe."

"Oh, so we're really gonna talk about this now? Is that what you think happened? I know what happened, and it had nothing to do with me cutting you out."

"Because you know everything, right? You know the 'word of God'."

"You have an illness. You've allowed your soul to be corrupted with this perverse sexualization, and then you put blasphemous ideas into Mom's head. You sunk the devil's claws into her so far that it was impossible to rid her mind of such immense brain rot. You turned your back on God and so she did the same."

"I didn't turn my back on shit. I spent years wondering what was wrong with me. Listening to ridiculous sermons about the role of a man and a woman and protesting same-sex marriages until one day I realized this just is who I am. I don't need a book to tell me how to be. I've received more love and compassion from the people I know now than I ever did from that church."

"The church was always there for you."

"They *shunned* me. I know you couldn't possibly have any idea how that feels, but let me paint a picture. They saw me on the street and spit on my shoes. Called me a hellspawn. A groomer. A pedophile. A fucking pedophile, Joe. One woman who used to smile at me in church all of a sudden turned around and said she prayed for my demise. You know who never did that? Mom."

"She was confused."

"Oh, that's rich. She loved me—all of me. I showed her my true self, and she loved me the same. And that just drove you crazy, didn't it?"

"She *chose* you!" Joe screamed, his frustration evacuating his lungs.

Silence.

"That's what this has all been about?" Anthony said. "You think she chose me over you?"

Joe didn't respond.

"She never had a crisis of faith," Anthony said.

"Yes, she did. I saw it. Before she died, almost every night, I saw a woman in flames beggin' for her soul to be saved. And I was helpless to save her. Once I realized it was Mom ... it was too late. But then I saw *you* in flames beggin' for *your* soul to be saved. God Himself is telling me to save you. I might be the only person who can. I can't leave another soul wasted in the depths of Hell."

"What are you talking about? That's complete nonsense."

"I won't ask you to reject your homosexuality. That's something we can work on. But I won't let you leave until you've accepted Jesus Christ as your Lord and Savior."

Anthony rolled his eyes. "I didn't do shit to Mom. I'm not contagious, dumbass. Mom never stopped believing. If there is a Heaven, she's there, and if there was ever an example to live by, it was hers. What's your example?"

The remainder of the ride was quiet. They got to a basketball court and changed on opposite sides of the truck, concealing themselves behind the heavy doors. They ran and dribbled and shot and dropped sweat onto the cement, but it wasn't how it used to be when they were younger. It wasn't that they were out of shape and hadn't touched a basketball in years. The fun of playing a brotherly game was an alien concept to them.

They felt more distant than they'd ever had, but they didn't discuss it. They played through it. The less said, the better at that point.

The silence weighed heavy on Anthony, who had assumed he'd come away from this experience apathetic to Joe's existence. But he was beginning to wonder what his story would even be. Whether this all was a sad waste of time.

A sobering study of a man taught to hate and call it love.

Three Hours Before Deworming

Anthony had known of the disappearance of Trisha McCann. It wasn't a national news story, but part of his research heading into the trip involved a scan of local headlines, with a specific interest in missing person cases.

Trisha's aunt was a known member of the Fellowship of the First Divine. Her vanishing act left no trace behind, no leads or suspects. Her aunt publicly requested that the public pray for her "nephew," something news articles had to correct with an explanation of how Trisha identified. Some things change; some stay the same.

Anthony followed Joe into the house, donning a sweat-soaked t-shirt.

A petite figure stood next to Darla in the kitchen with their back to Anthony.

"Oh, we have another guest?" Joe said.

JOEY POWELL

"Sure do," Darla replied. "Look who the cat dragged in."

A teenager with a pale face and freckles turned around, sporting a short, parted haircut, khakis, and a linen blazer. It was Trisha McCann, a missing person standing before Anthony in the flesh.

He was forced to hide his surprise. Since the story didn't get wide coverage, everyone in the room would presume he was unaware of it.

Joe expressed the shock instead. "Darla, that's ... That's Trisha McCann."

"Tristan, actually," the teen said. "The confusion is warranted."

"Wait ... What's happening?" Anthony asked.

"She went missing a week ago."

Darla cut Joe down with her eyes. "Joe ... *his* name is Tristan."

Emphasis on *his*. For some reason, Trisha was allowing it.

Anthony made a quick attempt to break the tension, moving in for a handshake. "Well, Tristan," he said, feeling weird about it, "it's nice to meet you. I'm Anthony, Joe's brother and Darla's favorite brother-in-law."

The teen's smile widened, but their eyes were glazed over, giving an eerie appearance like an android learning a new emotion. "It's nice to meet you as well, Anthony."

"Do the authorities know you—" Joe was interrupted.

"Tristan has asked that we respect his privacy for now," Darla said.

"This has been all over the news. We have to tell—"

"Even from his parents. Now, we're almost finished preparing dinner. You boys go make yourselves presentable."

Anthony shared a glance with Joe, feeling their brains interlock, bonding in the feeling that something was very wrong. They'd just rewound the clock fifteen years, baring a connection in a way that only siblings can. Joe wasn't someone he could trust, but the glance gave him a glimmer of hope that someday he could.

The rumors of conversion therapy were unavoidable in Anthony's research of the Fellowship. Now, Trisha McCann goes missing for a week near a White nationalist church, comes back referring to herself as Tristan. The ploy was so achingly obvious that Anthony could have dunked his head in a vat of acid and screamed until every synapse in his brain expired. There was a sadness in Trisha's eyes that was raw and palpable, and Anthony refused to think of her as anything other than who she was when she was kidnapped. *She* was *Trisha* McCann. Not this person the Fellowship had made her.

Anthony wasn't out to save anyone before, but he had stumbled upon a new incentive to burn the Fellowship down.

The sun hung low in the living room window, casting a golden haze over the woods. Anthony sat at the table opposite Trisha, with one hand held in Joe's, the other in Darla's.

Darla led the blessing, thanking God for all the processed prepackaged rolls that had been shipped in eighteen-wheelers to the local Harris Teeter. "Thank you, God, for showing Tristan the path to us. We are so glad to have him join the Fellowship and contribute to our community in a way fitting of your glory. As always, we thank you for your grace. Amen."

Tristan. There it was again, stinging Anthony's ears. His mouth opened to correct Darla, but he shut it quickly. Everyone said "Amen" except Anthony.

"That was beautiful, Darla. Thank you," Trisha said. "I'm very happy to know good people like you."

Darla gave her an "Oh, shucks" kind of look, and Anthony could have vomited on the table.

Each of them started filling their plates, with Anthony following their lead instinctively. Though he'd prepared himself for the worst aspects of the Fellowship, seeing their cruelty materialize in front of him, the Stepford Wives empty smile of a child having experienced a change he was certain she hadn't wanted, left him without much of an appetite.

"So, Anthony, Darla tells me you're a writer," Trisha said.

Anthony's brain fired quickly, searching for any instance within the past thirty-six hours in which he told Darla this. Had she been looking into him? All of his online content was under a pseudonym, and she'd have to dig deep to find any connection to him.

It took all the willpower and strength in his neck to not look in Darla's direction, hoping his expectation of a "gotcha" expression wouldn't become a reality.

"I dabble a fair amount, sure," Anthony said. "Mostly dumb clickbait stuff."

"Oh, wow. You always wanted to be a writer," Joe said. "Good for you. Back in our grade school days, this guy used to write these cool, like, fantasy stories, if I remember correctly"

"Yeah, you're a big fantasy reader now, right?"

"What? I'm not really a—"

"It's not quite fantasy these days," Anthony continued. "But it's a living."

"That's great, though," Trisha said. "That's your passion. I used to wanna be a writer."

"Used to?"

"Well, I suppose I still do. But the things I used to write about, you know—witchcraft, demons, that sort of stuff—I had to let go of all that."

"Why's that?" Anthony asked her.

"False idols," Darla answered instead.

"From ... witchcraft?" Anthony asked.

"'You shall have no other gods before me'," Darla quoted.

"It's ... literally fiction, though."

"Hey, Tristan," Joe interrupted, "when did you, uh ... return?"

Goddammit, Joe, Anthony thought, the deadname curling in his ear.

"Just today. I was taking some time to build my connection to the Lord."

The fuck? Anthony's head exploded.

"What happened while you were gone?" Joe asked.

Trisha gave him that same vacant, uncanny smile. Somewhere down below her lips and past her teeth, there was something dormant, stuck in a sleep-like trance. "I told you. I was building my relationship with God."

"Why are you calling yourself a different name now?" Anthony asked.

Darla cut in. "He's always been—"

"I think we should give this perfectly capable human being a chance to answer, don't you?" Anthony'd had to keep things cordial with Darla before, but his meter for patience was about to tip over.

"He's been confused," Darla said. "He's been confused because he allowed himself to become detached from the word of God. Boys are not girls. Girls are not boys. To think anything different, well ... that's not really living in God's image, is it?"

"What's God's image?" Anthony asked.

"God created man and woman. Adam and Eve."

"No, God created Adam. Adam got bored, and God removed a rib then—*poof*—Eve appeared." He turned to Joe. "I have all my ribs, don't you?"

"'A woman must not wear men's clothing'," Darla said, "'or a man wear women's clothing—'"

"'For the Lord your God detests anyone who does this.' I'm familiar. I don't think the Old Testament has a monopoly on fashion trends, doll." He could have gone all night with this. Every fire and brimstone passage was seared into the inner linings of his skull, an imprint he was forced to carry with him forever.

Trisha was caught in the crossfire, silently cutting through pieces of meat on her plate while her fake smile slid down, down, down.

Joe cut in. "Could you both please ..." He collected himself. "Darla, we have a missing person in our house. We need to call the parents."

"There's no need for that now," Darla said, practically asking Anthony to throw her through the window.

"You could be accused of kidnapping," Anthony added as a threat more than anything else.

"What do *you* want, Trisha?" Anthony asked directly.

Darla blurted. "His name is—"

Anthony silenced her with a finger. "Let her speak!"

SQUIRMING ALL THE WAY UP

The room fell silent as Trisha's teeth ground a piece of meat. She closed her eyes, swallowed, and inhaled. "It's like a voice in my head has been asleep all this time, and now it's awake. It's buried that other side of me. The ... sinful side." A tear formed in the corner of her closed eye. "Deep, deep down." She opened her eyes, causing the tear to fall. A smile rose on her face, and the tear rose with it. "I'll call my parents after dinner—I promise. Right now, I just want to enjoy this lovely—" Suddenly, she gagged. "I'm sorry. Excuse—"

It happened again. This time, she grabbed her stomach, first with one hand, then with both.

"Something wrong with the food?" Darla asked.

Something sloshed from under the table, coming from Trisha's direction.

The layer of serenity peeled itself from Trisha's face as her insides growled. Her eyes found Darla. "Is this normal?"

"Are you having a stomachache, dear?" Darla asked. For a moment, her eyes met Anthony's, an instant of panic wedged within her calm demeanor.

Trisha screeched. "I can feel them!"

She fell from her chair, landing hard on her shoulder and causing Joe and Anthony to jump out of their seats. Anthony sped over to Trisha as she curled into a ball on the floor.

"Get them out!" she yelled.

A small, bony hand gripped Anthony's shoulder. "Get away from him!" Darla yelled. "It will pass!"

"Get what out?" Anthony asked the pain-stricken teen as Darla tried and failed to pull him backward.

Trisha said something at such a low volume he couldn't make it out. A second hand gripped his free shoulder. He brushed it off and leaned in close with his ear to Trisha's mouth.

Trisha whispered, "The worms."

Joe ripped Anthony off of Trisha's side. "Let's give him some air," he said.

Anthony backed away on his palms and heels as Trisha let out a series of screams. Had he heard her right? *The worms. The worms. The worms.* It played over and over in his head, twirling like a carousel of absurdity.

Finally, the screams quieted. Trisha settled. Her breathing normalized.

"I'm okay now, I think," she said. Quite casually, she lifted herself up and readjusted the chair. "Oh, I apologize. I sure made a mess of things, didn't I?"

"You gave us quite a fright," Darla said.

"Yeah," Anthony said. *The worms. The worms. The worms.* "Quite the fright."

Trisha sat back down at the table and tucked her chair in with a couple quick scoots. It was as if a switch had flipped and everything was back to whatever version of normal this was for her.

"Thank you," Trisha said. "I'm glad Father Henry wasn't around to see that. He sure has seen me at my worst these past few days."

Wait, what? Anthony thought. *That old guy with the priest collar?*

A similar look of shock flashed across Joe's face as well.

"You've been with Pastor Henry?" Joe said.

"The lawn care guy?" Anthony added.

"Lawn Care guy?" Trisha said.

SQUIRMING ALL THE WAY UP

"That's enough, boys. Let's enjoy the meal now." Darla went back to her seat and slid her chair in.

Anthony and Joe returned to the table with the pretense of normality.

Trisha's mom came and picked her up later that night—or at least that's who Darla said she called to pick Trisha up. Anthony wasn't sure he believed anything Darla said at that point.

Anthony helped Joe clear the table as Darla occupied herself outside with Trisha and whoever the visiting driver was.

"Some bullshit's going on with that child, and we need to figure out what it is," Anthony whispered to Joe.

"The boy seems happy."

"She's not a *boy,* dammit. The church did something to that kid, and that old pastor has something to do with it."

"Why is it so hard to believe that—"

"I swear, if you say something about God's grace or miracles, I will put you down where you stand. You *know* what's going on; I know you do."

"It looks to me like Tristan went looking for God and found Him," Joe said. "Don't be afraid."

"Afraid of what?

"I believe in time, you'll find Him too." Joe gave Anthony a satisfied grin. "He's reunited with his family now. Don't ruin this for him."

Anthony stared inquisitively at the thing that used to be his brother. Any flashes of his old self were long gone, his faith overriding any natural sense of caution.

The door opened. Darla just always seemed to be there when Anthony wanted her around the least.

"I wish you all had made Tristan feel a bit more comfortable," Darla said.

"Sorry, honey," Joe replied. "It was just surprising is all. I'm glad to see Tristan is doin' better."

"Better?" Anthony repeated.

"Better. Yes." All five feet of Darla looked primed to pounce on Anthony then. "Well, I'm going to go get ready for bed. Joe, did you run by the grocery store today?"

"Aw, dangit, I forgot," Joe said. "Anthony, you wanna make a grocery run with me?"

Anthony's fingertips tingled, itching to rip open the latch on the door of the shed, which seemed to whisper to him fifty yards from where he stood. "I'm pretty wiped, actually. And I need to catch up on some emails."

"I'll be in my room if you need anything," Darla said.

Anthony gave her an unenthusiastic thumbs up. The two of them alone on the property? So many things could go wrong. But then again, he was a bit of a master at navigating situations anyone could deem "wrong." The neo-Nazi group he infiltrated and stole incriminating assassination plans from? Very wrong.

See, at that very moment, Anthony knew two things for certain: first, Trisha had been presumed missing but had spent time with Father Henry all along; second, there had been a scream in the woods, followed by a sighting of Father Henry near the vicinity of the scream shortly after.

Thirty-Three Minutes Before Deworming

Anthony waved Joe off as he watched the truck rumble down the driveway and out of view. With Darla occupied in the bedroom, it was time for him to explore.

He retraced his steps back to the wooden shed, zigzagging through trees and using his cell phone flashlight to illuminate the path.

The lock was undone on the latch, dangling from its rounded arch, unlike how he'd last seen it that very morning.

Anthony looked behind him and listened for footsteps. A quick burst of a thought crossed his mind that he'd stumbled upon a trap, that someone intuited his curiosity and wanted him to pull back the door of that shed. Regardless, it was a golden opportunity.

He slid the lock off the latch and opened the shed door slowly, careful to dull the friction of the rusted hinges.

Sure enough, the only items inside were lawn equipment (a push mower, shovels, rakes, hoes) and gardening tools lining the wooden shelves (twine, cutters, a pick axe). A square rug lay in the center of the shed, occupying the majority of the floor space and matted with years of dust and grass and grime from the equipment on top of it.

Taking a careful scan of the shelves, something caught Anthony's eye. A metal block roughly four inches wide, the light of his phone revealing two knobs at the top, one with a plus sign and the other with a negative.

A car battery.

"No way," he said in disbelief.

He backed up toward the center of the shed, stopping when his steps were met with a hollow *thud*. He looked down at the rug below him and gave it another stomp. No foundation underneath. Just air on the underside of the flooring.

Anthony reached down and pulled one corner of the rug back, revealing the edges of a hidden door.

Jackpot.

After rearranging the lawn equipment to one corner of the shed, he pulled the rug over far enough to uncover the door completely, then lifted the door until it stood at a right angle, creating a black opening. The flashlight showed him a short wooden stairwell.

"Hello?" he called out.

No answer.

He cautiously placed a heel down each wooden step, counting seven in total. A stale chemical stench filled his lungs, smelling like cleaning supplies had been spilled on the surface of the pit.

He reached the bottom and waved his phone around the edges of a dark cellar four times the size of the shed, with stone walls paved around the edges and bottom. His light found a switch along the wall next to the cellar entrance. When he flipped it, strips of bolted, buzzing lights along the ceiling brought the cellar to life.

SQUIRMING ALL THE WAY UP

A pair of chains were drilled into the back wall, their shackles open. A metal chair sat at the center of the room. Pressed against the left wall was a cheap-looking foldout table with steel legs and a Bible, a notepad, and a pencil on top of it. Stacks upon stacks of old, worn-out books with papers spilling like guts out of them leaned against the desk.

Anthony peered above the table to see a grid of pictures—five-by-sevens of men and women, boys and girls, terrified and bruised. He scanned the pictures from left to right—

Until his eyes stopped on Trisha, her hair down to her shoulders, signifying an earlier time, perhaps mere days ago. Her eyes hung low to the floor with a solemn look of defeat on her face, washed in the harsh light of a camera flash.

Anthony's hands moved as quickly as his mind could command them, snapping pictures of the portraits, the chains, the books, careful not to move anything out of place. As far as he was concerned, this was a crime scene.

Centered against the right wall was a rolling metal cart with a single shelf. A heavy-looking, dusty 1990s TV sat on top of it, connected with a crudely twisted rope of cords to a VHS player beneath it. At the mouth of the VCR sat the black lip of a VHS tape, patiently waiting to be inserted.

The tape called to him, and he wondered how far he could get from the property on foot with it before anyone knew it was gone. How far would he have to run until he got decent reception?

He reached out to grab the tape.

But was halted by a hissing sound at the far end of the room.

Not quite a hissing sound, he thought. More like a long wheezing exhale, like a large cloud of air deflating from a pair of obstructed lungs.

Anthony turned back and eyed the far wall again. In the bottom left corner of the room was a circular opening leading to a haphazardly chiseled tunnel that stretched beyond what the cellar lights could expose. It seemed to be emitting the sound. He inched closer, his heart rattling in his chest, for a moment allowing himself to forget that every second was precious, that at any moment, he could be discovered.

He walked past the metal chair and brushed a shackle with his foot, gazing into the corner pocket. Someone—or some*thing*—was in there, breathing in the darkness.

The hissing stopped.

For a moment, it seemed like the only thing accompanying him in the room was his own breathing.

Until a black mass flopped out of the hole and landed at his feet, so grotesque and uncanny that it made Anthony's body seize. The worm-like creature slapped against the surface of the cellar, dispersing a black slime like tar that spattered against Anthony's ankles. Through the creature's thin skin, Anthony could see its shifting insides, ground meat colored in the gaseous, bursting colors of the cosmos. Something beautiful wrapped in something hideous.

Anthony sprang back, stumbled on his heels, and fell to the ground, too afraid to scream. He watched as the creature wiggled and slapped the ground, this eyeless, shapeless thing that challenged his perception of life, science, and everything he knew.

It came closer, hissing and wheezing as if sniffing for Anthony.

SQUIRMING ALL THE WAY UP

Finally, the feeling returned to Anthony's hands and legs, and he bolted, running up the stairs and slamming the cellar door shut. He piled shovels, bags of potting soil, and anything else in reach atop the door, hoping to pin the worm inside.

He grabbed the car battery off the shelf—*his* battery—preparing to make a mad dash back through the woods.

Just then, he felt a prick in the left side of his neck, so sudden that it might've been a bee sting. He grabbed the entry point and caught the tail end of a needle sliding out.

Damn, he thought. *She got me.*

He turned to see a shadowy figure standing in the doorway, a petite frame swallowed by the aged lumber surrounding it, with the faint outline of a syringe in its hand.

"What did you just do?" Anthony asked with a palm against his neck.

"What has gotten into you, Anthony?" Darla said in an exaggerated tone, feigning concern. "We were just getting to know each other."

"And it's been a magical and fascinating experience," Anthony said. Blood seeped from his neck because of the way he had bucked against the needle. He hoped his reaction was fast enough to keep some of Darla's cocktail out.

Still, he had to hightail it out of there before whatever was in him took effect. He lowered his shoulder and bowled into Darla, satisfyingly sending her flopping to the ground on the other side of the shed like a pancake.

With Darla out of the way, he tried to traverse the woods with the little moonlight he had to work with. He reached for his phone to call Joe as a shade of drowsiness lowered in his vision. He was slipping, the feeling of the ground against his feet fading, the tips of his fingers numbing. He needed to call Joe before he went under.

Then he remembered how pointless getting through to Joe had served him. For all he knew, Joe was in on this too.

His legs hobbled and buckled.

He collided with a tree, a blow that rattled his brain and shook the whole world out of existence.

Everything went black.

Eighteen Minutes Before Deworming

Anthony's eyes opened.

He was stripped down to his undershirt, lying on his back. His wrists were suspended in the air, shackled with the thick chains he had been on the other side of seemingly moments before.

Every subtle movement caused an unbearable quaking vibration above his eyes.

He sat up, resting his back against the stone wall, eyeing the dingy cellar.

Sitting in the metal chair before him was a kid in a black robe, looking like a high schooler who went to a party as a pastor. It took a moment for Anthony to realize that the mustache on the pimple-faced kid wasn't fake. A pair of reading glasses sat atop his nose as he scanned over a Bible with the glee of a teenager reading a dirty magazine.

SQUIRMING ALL THE WAY UP

Anthony pulled against the chains, testing their strength. The rattle prompted the kid to hold up a finger as if to say, "Just a moment," seemingly having found a *really* good passage.

"Fuck are you?" Anthony said.

The pastor removed his eyes from the book and smiled. "Father Castor."

"What are you, twelve? You're no father of mine, buddy."

"You should consider yourself lucky to be down here, boy."

The Southern drawl was making Anthony seriously miss the city.

"I don't think anyone's called themselves lucky being chained to a goddamn wall—"

"You bite your tongue. You take the Lord's name in vain and it's like daggers piercing my ears." Castor stood quickly, the metal chair sliding against the stone underneath him. He held the Bible with two hands as if the thing were at risk of being dropped. "I see you met the All-Father a bit early. He seems eager to explore your mind. Don't worry, you'll see him again soon. I just had to remind him that we do things a certain way down here."

"Is that what you call the little worm monster? What is that thing?"

"Don't be crude. He is neither worm nor monster. He is a gift. Our salvation."

Black liquid traced the worm's path as it had thrashed around, searching blindly for Anthony in the last few seconds he was down there. Anthony's heart rate spiked as panicked thoughts occupied his mind as to what the thing would do to him once it found him. He imagined the black goo all over his body, the thin skin encasing a rolling maze of stars suffocating him.

"You must be very confused," Castor said.

"Very astute," Anthony responded.

"Such a smart alec. The McCann boy had a tongue like a whip too. But the All-Father fixed him. And He'll fix you."

Boy. Him. There it was again.

Father Castor gripped the corner of the rolling cart with the old TV on top of it. He wheeled it closer to Anthony, an orange extension cord straightening as he did. The tape hanging in the opening of the VCR player was a reminder of the possibilities Anthony could have afforded himself had he been a bit faster.

With the cart at the center of the room, Anthony had a clear view over the top of the TV, where a black dome hung on the ceiling with a black pupil at the center of it. Maybe Darla had been watching him.

Maybe getting captured was simply an inevitability.

"This will explain everything," Castor said. He pressed the power button on the TV, then bent down, squealing the way old men do, and pushed the tape into the VCR. Mechanical sounds whirled from the VCR as it accepted the tape. The screen became blue, then tracking lines cut across it until it went black.

Castor repositioned the metal chair, angling it for a better view.

A weathered man appeared on screen, with skin like old leather and a long white beard and a white suit, heavily saturated in bright pixels, giving off a '90s digital camera quality. Anthony recognized the house behind him as Darla's, and he recognized the man from Darla's wall.

The man spoke with a smile and a thick and cheery Southern accent. "Hello there. I am Anders Johanson, and you are but one of the very few people who have been selected to join the Fellowship and inherit the fruits that come with it. Take a walk with me."

SQUIRMING ALL THE WAY UP

A cheesy digital wipe flashed across the screen, transitioning to a shot of Johanson walking toward the camera along the side of the house. "Centuries ago, a group of Viking warriors dominated a village and stumbled upon a secret that the fallen locals died protecting. Inside a cave deep in the mountains of Norway, they found something not of terrestrial origin. The being could only survive by spreading its seed. But in order to multiply, the offspring needed warm hosts to live inside. The villagers, meek little souls they were, had been dying off, and therefore so, too, was the being."

Another transition, this time a star expanding from the center to the edges of the screen. Johanson stood in front of the freshly painted shed.

"Understanding their mission of purity and recognizing the Vikings' immense strength of mind and body, the being had found suitable hosts for its offspring. But Vikings, you see ... don't do anything without compensation.

"The warriors made a deal with the being. His offspring would bond with them, and he would show the soldiers the path to their eternal glory. You see, the being saw beyond what any terrestrial entity can comprehend, leading the soldiers to countless victories, exposing the weaknesses of each village as the Vikings swept through Norway. Finally, their mission of supremacy was within reach, and the being was stronger than ever. They had found God."

Castor sniffled and wiped a tear with his sleeve.

Johanson continued. "After years of bonding, it became clear the All-Father would only bond with beings of Nordic descent and reject those without it. When the offspring attempted to bond with their slaves, the worms would die near instantaneously, causing the bodies of the slaves to decay from the inside out. The All-Father doesn't communicate in the same way you and I do, but it was clear that he needed the strength of Viking descendants."

The screen wiped to a tracking shot inside the church, following the shaky old man as he walked backward down the carpet separating the rows of pews.

"Some years ago, I relocated Him here and began the Fellowship of the First Divine, bringing with me other descendants who were chosen by the All-Father to lead the human race. He has gifted us with ultimate knowledge. Knowledge of our enemies and knowledge of those who could steer us toward righteous glory. He has chosen us. And now it is time to see if He has chosen you."

Johanson stopped at the foot of the stage, with the podium in the background above his shoulder.

"You see, the All-Father requires hosts to live, to continue to endow us with His invaluable gifts. In order for Him to persevere, we, too, must create offspring for Him to bond with. If you are watching this, it is because you are impure of faith but perhaps not of heritage. It may take some time, but the All-Father will rectify these impurities. He will ensure that you're able to carry out your biological responsibility. To create a perfect race of human beings representative of God Himself.

"You are so very welcome for this gift you are about to receive. All hail the All-Father. Take a moment to pray with me."

The man on the screen bowed his head in prayer.

Anthony looked over at Castor, who had taken the command from a man long dead very seriously and had his head bowed as well. Anthony's eyes darted from the shackles to the stairs, trying to conjure up an escape plan, but feeling helpless.

SQUIRMING ALL THE WAY UP

"Now," Johanson raised his head and continued, "your assigned pastor will guide you through the next steps in the bonding process. I greatly look forward to having you join our perfect race and contributing to our ideal world, which we'll continue to create in the All-Father's image. God bless."

Johanson stared at Anthony with yellow teeth, nodding with a crazed grin. The screen went black.

Castor sniffled again, took his glasses off, and wiped tears from his eyes, so touched by the dead man's words. Anthony wondered how many times the pastor had seen it and how many times he'd done so knowing that someone in his presence was about to be violated.

Castor rolled the TV cart back to the far corner of the room next to the stairs, then walked slowly toward Anthony, collecting himself after a sobbing fit. He breathed in deeply, grinning with his hands on his hips.

"I suppose now you're going to tell me what this 'bonding process' is?" Anthony asked.

"It's very simple. The All-Father comes through that hole, then secretes His offspring. They find their way into your mouth, and if they accept you, well … they start their long journey up to your brain. You may fight it at first. There may be some discomfort, but that fades once they begin traveling upward."

Anthony thought of the black worm. He thought of several smaller black worms invading his esophagus, diving down his throat, and burrowing into his intestines. How would they even get into his brain? Would they chew through his stomach lining, ripping pounds of flesh and organs, squirming all the way up?

Then he thought of Trisha McCann. He imagined her in the cellar, watching the same video, getting the same explanation from a teary-eyed pastor. That scream in the woods Anthony had heard was her—he was sure of it. She called out for someone to save her, and he had failed to intervene.

"I know you're frightened by what you've seen, but know that our encounters with God are never what we expect. This is a good thing. The All-Father will help you see the path forward. You will procreate, and you will save others, just as we are savin' you."

"Save me from what?" Anthony asked.

"Those who would ruin our cause."

"You'll find out soon enough how fast I can ruin your cause," Anthony promised.

"I'll leave you to it then, son. And Anthony ... I'm really looking forward to seein' the man you become. Darla is as well. As you know, she and Joe have had trouble conceiving, but you ... she's hopin' you might bring us a strong child to raise into the Fellowship."

Are you fucking kidding me?

"And don't worry about the bonding process. All-Father took to Joe very well. That's how we knew you would be a perfect fit. We've lost so many souls to faulty bonding." He gave a careless sigh, then turned and walked up the stairs and out of Anthony's sight, closing the door with a hard *thunk*.

All was quiet.

Then something hissed.

In just a few seconds, he'd be staring down the worm from another world, fighting for his life as it attempted to impregnate him.

But as long as Anthony had teeth, not one of those things would get inside his mouth.

Not a single one.

CHAPTER FIVE

Fifty-Two Minutes After Deworming

"Is that you, Anthony?" Joe thought he said out loud. It sounded like he was in a fishbowl, and he honestly couldn't tell if it was in his head.

Joe's vision was blurry, and he felt as weak as he remembered feeling before he passed out, but if he could still talk, it meant he was still alive.

"Settle down, now. It's okay," someone said from his right side.

"Anthony?" Joe asked just to make sure.

"Yeah," the voice said. "Yeah, it's Anthony."

Joe could barely hear him. "Where are we, Ant?"

"We're in the hospital," the voice said. "You've been mumblin' a bit. Sayin' you got some things you need to tell me."

"Is it really you?" Joe said. "I can't see too good right now."

"Rest your eyes, Joe," the voice said. "You just tell me whatever it is you wanna tell me about those worms."

Twenty-Five Minutes Before Deworming

With the sticky summer wind flowing into his truck window, Joe's head buzzed over the interaction with the McCann kid. Several thoughts wrestled in his brain. The loudest parts told him Tristan's discovery of the Lord was a miracle, clear as days, but a deeper part of him, something quiet and nagging, remembered the frighteningly unconvincing smile, the sudden outburst of pain, causing him to consider the teen was unwell.

But each time he created that opening within himself to consider it, a thousand voices would shout that God made two genders, a symphony of shrieks declaring a boy can't just switch to a girl. The voices asked him to question what damage the adults are causing the next generation if they're raised with no foundation for their own identity.

Parents are forcing hormone replacement therapy on eight-year-olds. And this is what we get.

Teachers are forcing gender ideology on preschool kids. Where will it end?

Same-sex marriage is eroding traditional family values.

We must stop them before they corrupt our children.

Save the children, Joe.

They weren't the sounds of righteousness but rather the sounds of fear. Joe loved God but feared him all the same. He could love his neighbor and fear their influences as well.

He could love Tristan.

Just as he feared Trisha.

A baby's cry quieted the anger in him, redirecting his thoughts to something he perceived to be real. The crying was faint like a whisper—or as faint as a baby's cry could be. With nothing but high beams to guide his way, Joe hung his head out the window, hearing the cries fade in.

He raised his foot off the gas pedal, looking ahead at the oval of light shining against the asphalt.

The beams captured the brown-haired woman all at once, the bottom of her white dress swaying with the summer breeze, holding the baby in her arms as it cried out.

Joe had always seen the woman from a distance. He used to fear the ghosts that haunted his psyche, reminding him of his sins. But he was now deputized with a sense of divine purpose. He had seen God and was ready to confront the Devil. The brunette—what was her name?—was a soul that he was meant to save.

Long brown hair flapped around the sides of the woman's face, surrounding a head that was smooth like a mannequin over the crying child. Joe stared at the featureless face in a daze as the woman clutched the baby to her chest.

The baby stopped crying.

The short moment of silence was broken by pained, agonizing moans. Though she had no mouth to yell with, the woman's head dispersed the warped sound.

Cold fingertips surrounded Joe's scalp.

He swiveled his head to see a set of arms with charred skin swinging from the eye sockets of his mother's face, the white liquid of her eyes smeared around the forearms like explosions of wet paint.

Joe swiped at the vision of his mother and put all of his weight on the gas, attempting to put the revenants of his past in the rearview.

His mother melted out of his periphery.

Eventually, Joe lowered his speed, the surge of his heart coming down as well.

Twelve Minutes Before Deworming

Joe got out of his car in the Harris Teeter parking lot. His truck was one of a few vehicles occupying the blacktop, which was barely lit by a few buzzing lampposts.

He didn't think much of the black van that pulled up behind him until he heard a sliding door grind open.

A flurry of arms swept him off the ground before he could turn.

A black sack flew over his head.

Zip ties squeezed his wrists together.

His world shifted as the hands shoved him into the van. Two seconds later, the door slid and shut.

The engine revved.

"What—what—what," Joe muttered in fright.

"Don't talk, Joe," a soft voice said. "We're not going to hurt you. Let's just ... not make this weird by talking while you have a bag over your head. We'll get to our destination soon, and then we'll talk. Sound good?"

"Uh ... Yeah, I guess." They knew his name, so he must have been somewhat important.

An overwhelming calm spread through Joe. He remembered that God had a plan for him.

And God had veto power.

Two Minutes Before Deworming

Joe felt a sudden chill before his mask came off.

It was a meat locker. Slabs of severed animal flesh hung upon hooks, slowly twisting in suspension.

Joe couldn't see who was behind him as their hands pushed him forward. The red, skinless slabs zipped past him.

"Someone 'bout to tell me what's goin' on?" he said as his feet shuffled forward, his wrists against his tailbone.

"We're trying to help you, okay? We just don't have much time." It was that same soft voice again.

The person it belonged to pushed Joe toward a nine-foot rectangular chamber with a clear glass pane and long metal handle. Beyond the glass was a white interior lit in a blue glow.

A short guy in a jean jacket ran past Joe and opened up the door of the chamber. "Are we sure he's infected?" the jean jacket guy said.

"He's married to Patrice Johanson. He definitely is," the voice behind him said.

SQUIRMING ALL THE WAY UP

Joe stiffened his legs, trying to slow his momentum. "Who the hell is that? I don't know what you're plannin' on doin', but I'm not goin' in that thing."

"Sorry," the voice said. "You know her as Darla Smithie."

Joe felt more hands on his back pushing against his resistance as he came closer to the chamber. Joe noticed a nozzle and a digital gauge next to the door. Jean Jacket took a bulky pair of snow gloves out of his back pocket.

"It's just a cryo-chamber, bro. People do it all the time," Jean Jacket said. "I need to put these gloves on so your fingers don't freeze off."

Joe bucked his head back, smacking his skull against whoever was behind him. Feeling the sudden freedom from resistance, he spun around to make a run for it, but was met with a dozen people blocking his path.

"I am a messenger from God Himself!" he yelled. "You'd be wise to let me pass!" They weren't from South Point; he knew that for certain. Their streetwear would have been more appropriate in some busy metropolitan area, and their skin was not the pale white that he was used to.

The next thing he knew, the barrel of a revolver was in his face, connected to the hand of a man he didn't recognize at first. He was tall, wearing a beanie, and had a wispy, incomplete beard.

It was the kid he'd confronted at the gas station, the one he'd told to stay the hell away from Anthony.

The kid must have seen that look of recognition because the first thing he said was, "Yeah. It's me. Your brother told me who he was staying with, so I put a tracker on your car. Just needed an opportunity to get you here. Tyson's the name."

"So this is the Pluralist Society," Joe said. "I figured you'd have higher numbers."

"The woman you know as Darla Smithie is very dangerous, Joe," the soft voice said. "We need your help in bringing her down."

"That's my wife you're talking about," Joe said.

A middle-aged woman dressed in loose black clothing with pulled-back hair split the crowd and stepped forward. She would have appeared unremarkable to Joe were it not for her striking resemblance to another Fellowship member he saw every week, Diana McCann. Her look was slightly off from her sister. Her cheekbones were more defined, her jaw was broader, and she had a look of pure wrath. This was Elle McCann, Tristan's mother.

"You aren't the only man she's seduced into this world, Joe," the woman said. "And she's not even the worst of it. The Fellowship is a sickness, and they won't stop until it spreads everywhere. The All-Father is not what you think it is."

Joe recoiled. "How do you know about that?"

"Have you done the bonding?" Tyson asked.

"What ... bonding?" Joe replied.

"She could have fed them to him without his knowledge," Elle said. "It's possible." She took another step toward Joe. "Do you know where my daughter is?"

"Your daughter?" Joe asked. "I saw Tristan just this evening. He's better. He's with his aunt now."

Elle grabbed Joe by the collar and pulled him toward her, close enough for him to feel the hot breath on her lips. "What the hell did they do to her? I swear to the god you pray to if I find out you had anything to—"

SQUIRMING ALL THE WAY UP

"Elle!" Tyson yelled. "We don't have a lot of time."

The pain of loss surged through Elle as she gripped handfuls of Joe's shirt. He was curious as to why she carried that pain. In his mind, her child had been saved. She released him, giving his chest a slight nudge as she backed away, seething through pressed teeth.

Tyson cocked the hammer back on his revolver. "Joe ... please get in the cryo-chamber. I promise we won't let anything happen to you. We just need to make sure you're clean."

The pair of snow gloves slapped Joe's chest.

"I'm gonna put these on you, okay?" Jean Jacket said. "This is one hundred percent safe."

He slid the gloves on, struggling to get the tops through the zip ties.

Joe took a look at the crowd, paying special attention to the gunman and Elle McCann. "Why do you want me gettin' in this thing? Just tell me."

"To freeze out the offspring," Tyson said.

"I meant tell me something that makes sense."

"Because if you don't, we'll make you," Elle said. "How's that?"

Joe shook his head, then turned. Jean Jacket opened the door of the chamber, and Joe stepped in. The door closed quickly behind him.

A few quick beeps sounded.

Joe waited.

A whirring sound sent a rush of cold air against Joe's head, the icy chill lowering and burrowing under his clothes. The gloves were useless—his fingers were turning to glaciers. This was as cold as Joe had ever been. All he could do was breathe through it as even his lungs felt coated in ice.

Jean Jacket tapped on the door and yelled, "It's only two minutes! You're gonna feel great after!"

Deworming

The first minute was the longest of Joe's life.

During the second minute, worms whined inside his skull.

A squirming motion ran across every groove in his brain, a thousand tiny itches he couldn't scratch. He wrestled with the zip ties, his hands desperate to reach his skull as the worms thrashed around underneath it. The screams of the worms felt like they were a part of him—a deep vibration spiking down his skeletal structure, a sharp hiss that made Joe want to remove his ability to hear.

"Get them out of my head!" Joe screamed as he slammed his head against the wall of the chamber.

"You're almost done, Joe!" Jean Jacket yelled. "Twenty seconds!"

For ten of those seconds, Joe felt like spiked, rusty gears were spinning in his head.

For the last ten, the hissing died down.

The machine stopped and the door opened.

Joe stumbled out and spilled onto the floor, lucky to not have dislocated the shoulder he landed on.

"What in God's name?! What in God's name?!" he kept yelling. "What did you do to me?!"

"Do you hear a screaming sound inside your head?" Tyson asked. "Do you feel anything moving around?"

"No!" he yelled. "I did, but I don't anymore. What the hell was that?!" His teeth clapped uncontrollably as shivers danced along his skin.

"Good," Tyson said as he threw a blanket over him. "It means the offspring are dead." He turned to Jean Jacket. "Cut him loose."

Jean Jacket flipped open a pocket knife and cut through the zip tie in one quick motion. Joe's hands rushed to the front of his body, covering his freezing chest with the corners of the blanket as he sat up on the floor.

"What was in my head?" Joe asked.

Tyson crouched down, getting his eyesight level with Joe's. "What you heard in your head was the offspring," he said. "It seems your wife hasn't been completely honest with you."

"Are you saying she put those things in my head?" Joe asked

"You would have had to consume them, but they burrow their way up into your brain. That's where they live. We just put you through the only reversing process we know of that works. The offspring thrive in heat. They can't survive in freezing temperatures. That's why they like it out here."

"So ... what happens now? Do they just stay in there all ... dead and whatnot?"

"Your body will dispose of them," Tyson said.

"You'll shit them out," Jean Jacket added.

"Now that you know the truth, we need you to help us," Elle said.

"Help you what?"

"For one, I want my goddamn daughter back," Elle said.

"And we need to kill the All-Father," Tyson said. "I think we can do both by exposing Patrice."

"You mean Darla? You're insane. She's my wife. *You're* the terrorists here."

"We don't have a lot of time here, Joe. I know you're cold as shit, but how does your head feel? Really think about it. Take any thought you typically have on a day-to-day basis. Tell me if you feel anything different."

So Joe did. His chattering had subsided, and his shivers were small tremors.

He gave himself a moment to rest.

"Allow me," Elle said, nudging Tyson on the shoulder. They switched places and Elle spoke softly to Joe. "My child came to me one day and told me they felt different. Before, I only thought of my child as a boy, but here they were, telling me not *what* they were, but *who* they truly were. Unlike so many children in the world, Trisha trusted me with her vulnerability, trusting that I would look past any learned notions of how the world works. I had a choice. Would I live with a child who would never trust me again? Who felt abandoned by my conditional love? Or would I prove to her that the world is a canvas for her to paint how she sees fit, that no one decides how she colors her canvas but her?

"Now ... having listened to that ... how do you feel?"

Joe's mind was clear. He wasn't overwhelmed by shouting phantoms telling him that hate was love and that fear was preservation. He didn't feel the needles of confusion of faith in his mind or the looming weight of the souls he couldn't take with him to the Kingdom.

Everything was so quiet. The influence of the All-Father had been stripped away like shedding skin.

"What did you do?" Joe asked.

"We got you better," Elle replied.

"And we can do it for so many people," Tyson said. "Right now, we need you to get your ass up."

"No one's going to believe this stuff."

"Oh, I'm intimately aware," Tyson said. "Once upon a time, I tried to ring the alarm. I was committed for the things I said. I had a low probability of bonding because, I mean … look at me. I escaped before the offspring took hold. What do you think happens to a sixteen-year-old orphan who cries wolf about an alien in an underground cellar? The Pluralist Society was able to get me deprogrammed. I've been free of the All-Father for three years."

"It's not just Trisha. People go missing in this area quite a bit," Elle said. "Those are the ones that don't bond. I don't think I have to spell out who those people are. We need to find out where the bodies are buried. Any evidence that can take the Fellowship down."

"You're asking me to snoop around to see if my wife's a murderer?"

"She pumped you full of alien organisms," Elle said. "My sister is a monster, but she talks enough to be useful. Ask Darla about the other men in her life before. According to Diana, none of them lasted very long and nobody has any idea where the hell they are."

Joe had left home that evening with an understanding of his purpose. The conflict he should have felt with the knowledge that his purpose was a lie was absent. The vitriolic side of him that demanded he defend his faith was no more. Instead, his faith was as uncertain to him as the circumstances that led him to Darla's home.

You aren't the only man she's seduced into this world, Joe, Elle had said. The statement lingered in his head like the chorus of a terrible song.

Twenty-Six Minutes After Deworming

Joe opened the front door with loops of grocery bags hanging from one hand. The thought of seeing his wife again, as if for the first time, was dragging him down. His stomach ballooned with dread. Opening the door was like crossing a threshold back into an unnatural world, one that he was forced to inhabit.

He shuddered at the sight of Darla staring straight at him from the kitchen table, thumbing through a smartphone.

"Hey, honey," he said, setting the groceries on the counter. "Where's Anthony?"

Darla took a stern tone. "Why don't you sit down?" She pointed to the chair beside her.

Joe walked toward the table and sat.

"Joe ... This might be hard for you to hear, but ... Your brother has deceived you."

"About ... what?" Joe said.

"He's not just a small-time internet writer. He's writing a piece about the Fellowship."

At that moment, everything made sense. The months of missed phone calls, the penetrating questions about the Fellowship. Anthony wasn't there to reconnect.

"I looked into his online presence," Darla continued. "Goes by a different name. He infiltrates religious and so-called 'far-right' movements with the sole purpose of humiliating them. He would have made a mockery of our people."

"Hm," Joe mumbled to himself, unsure of how to interpret his swirling emotions.

Darla quoted, "'And the devil, who deceived them, was thrown into the lake of burning sulfur, where the beast and the false prophet had been thrown. They will be tormented day and night forever ... and ever ...' Make no mistake, his deceit is the work of the devil." Darla slid the phone to Joe. "Look at this. You have to keep touching the screen or it'll go to sleep again."

Joe began reading what was on the screen. An email from Anthony's account sent the night before. Anthony had emailed someone about Joe's sleepwalking incident.

"He's been sending notes to his employer," Darla said.

Joe clicked through more emails.

"He's been writing about my, quote, 'eerie Biblical subservience,' and Lord knows what he would have said to exploit Tristan's recovery."

"Where is he?" Joe asked.

"Joe ..." She took his hand and stroked his palm. "Your brother is ... brainwashed. We just needed to scrub him clean."

"What are you ... Darla, where is he?" Joe asked again.

"You and I are perfect images of God's creation. Our purpose is to amass as many followers as we possibly can, to preserve a healthy, thriving lineage, and to excise any infection that would taint our message."

Thriving lineage. What was it that Elle had called her?

Johanson.

Patrice Johanson.

"I am the offspring of God," Darla said. "Same as you. He has shown me my purpose clear as day. My purpose was to meet you."

She smiled lovingly at Joe, and his stomach sank to the floor.

"You have no idea what's coming," Darla said. "One day, the White race will be extinct. Heterosexuals will be a minority. Christians will be put in detention centers, banished to rot away in a prison of our own inaction."

"Um ..." Joe stammered, unsure how to respond.

"I've seen it, Joe. If we stand by and let disgusting heathens like Anthony commit genocide of the White Christian race, this world—*His* perfect world—will fall into anarchy and chaos."

Joe stared at Darla in horror, seeing her full-tilt paranoia manifest in a way he'd never seen before. His lips quivered in search of a response that wouldn't come.

Darla calmed herself. "I know God has shown you things as well. He told you to bring Anthony to us. We must save Anthony. Because if we're unsuccessful, he will perish."

The front door flung open. The meek figure of Father Castor entered the living room. "Ah, Joe," he said. "Good to see you, son."

Son. Joe hated it even more now that he was dewormed.

Castor looked at Darla. "I take it he knows, then?"

SQUIRMING ALL THE WAY UP

Joe was so damn tired of being out of the loop he could have screamed.

"Not yet." Darla answered. "Joe, dear ... You wondered what the mark was, Joe. We all have it. It's how the All-Father talks to us." She slid her chair out from underneath her and turned with her back facing Joe. Her thin fingers clutched the hair dangling against her shoulders and pulled it down, causing the entirety of her wig to slide cleanly off.

In the middle of her bald head was the same purple orb Joe had seen on Father Castor's belly and on his own shoulder.

"As long as you've been in this house, honey," Darla said while facing away from Joe, "God has been with you."

"And He is with your brother now," Father Castor said. "The bonding process has begun."

Joe felt his insides shift again. It took every ounce of self-control within him to keep sour bile from launching onto the floor below him. He had to stay calm. He had to play the part.

"I believe ... I've always felt his presence here with me," Joe said, wincing at his own words. "I've felt it since you got me sober." *Since you fed me worms, all I've heard is noise and all I've felt is anger.* "What was it you told me, Father Castor? About God working in mysterious ways? Maybe Anthony was always supposed to be here." *Supposed to be assimilated.*

"You've made us very proud, son," Father Castor said.

Darla turned to face Joe. "So proud."

"I want to go see it happen," Joe said.

"You shouldn't interrupt the process," Father Castor replied.

"Then I'll be there when it's finished. I should go alone. He'll want to see me when it's done." Joe hoped they'd buy his sincerity.

Father Castor and Darla exchanged glances. Darla nodded.

"Of course, son," Father Castor said, stepping aside. "Go to the shed. You'll see a door in the center of the floor with stairs leading to a cellar." He raised a set of long, rusted keys. "To release him when the process is finalized."

Joe pulled the cellar door open and sped down the steps.

He was greeted by the repulsive and unbelievable image of Anthony kicking wildly at a giant worm, its thin skin and mushy flesh grotesque yet familiar. Anthony's hands were shackled to the stone wall, his wrists bloody from the struggle. Stripes of black liquid surrounded his arms and legs, leading to a radius of shiny dark slime and vomit around his mouth. He looked as if he'd been rolling in motor oil.

Then Joe got a clean view at the worm. Its backside disappeared into the corner of the cellar, and its front stood straight up like a cobra, with black liquid dripping from its underbelly.

The creature dove, and Anthony caught it between his thighs, stopping its slippery momentum. A small slit opened in its dark underside and propelled something that looked like a Silly String canister going dry. The debris slapped against Anthony's face and chest. The stuff started squirming atop Anthony's skin, and Joe realized what it was.

Goddamn worms.

"Joe!" Anthony yelled.

Anthony's scream shook Joe out of his daze. He took three quick steps and kicked at the worm, but his shoe slid right off the slippery skin. The thing was too damn wet to kick.

"Hang on," Joe said as he ran back up the stairs.

"Where are you going?!" Anthony yelled.

Joe grabbed the pick axe from the shed above and came back down. Noticing the axe, Anthony released the worm from his thighs, kicking and trying to roll away, mashing the smaller worms as he did. That gave Joe just enough room to ram the axe into the goopy monstrosity. It hissed and whined—a sound similar to what Joe had heard in the cryo-chamber.

The smaller worms screeched in a violent tone high enough to shatter glass. Joe's eardrums cracked against the sound as he yanked the axe back, ripping out a strand of black blood with bright yellow spots like stars intermingled within.

A harsh shriek came from above them—a high-pitched cry of pain. They each looked over to the stairwell, temporarily distracted from the scene around them.

The worm backed away, sliding into the hole at the corner of the cellar like a measuring tape retracting.

The smaller worms, seemingly lost of all direction, fell off of Anthony and flopped like fish on the ground, screaming incessantly.

Joe flicked and stomped the little bastards until they were all completely flat.

He took a moment to breathe as Anthony spat out a mixture of vomit and worm meat.

"What took you so long?" Anthony said.

"Got held up," Joe responded.

It was only then that Joe gave himself an opportunity to eyeball the contents of room—the chair, the desk, the TV stand, and the wall of photographs. All those souls, changed against their will, and some likely gone forever.

"What the fuck is going on, Joe?" Anthony said. "Did you know about this?"

"Of course I didn't know about this," Joe said, ripping his gaze away from the photographs and taking the keys out of his pocket. He bent down to Anthony and rammed each key into the shackles, trying to find a match. "Those things that are on the floor now? Yeah, they were in my goddamn head. I got 'em frozen out."

"What? When?"

Time was precious. Joe would explain everything later. "We have to get you out of here." He finally found the right key and twisted, freeing one of Anthony's wrists. "This is all so messed up. I'm sorry." He unlocked the second shackle. "How did you even get down here?"

"Your lovely wife drugged me and put me here," Anthony said.

Joe's entire body clenched.

Anthony continued. "Oh, and I'm pretty sure she swapped my car's battery out for a dead one."

"What? How would she have done that?"

"I don't know dick about cars. How am I supposed to know?"

A memory returned to Joe. A dead battery had caused his first interaction with Darla. There was no way it was a trick to force an interaction. That would have been too much of a coincidence.

Then again, he had seen and witnessed a lot of impossible shit that day.

"I'm sorry I got you into this," Joe said.

"Well, now your wife knows." Anthony pointed at the camera. "Smile. You're on TV."

This'll be an awkward goddamn conversation.

As Anthony wiped the puke and slime from his skin, Joe walked over for a closer look at the wall of faces, hypnotized by the despair the Fellowship had captured. "Still think Trisha's in a better place?" Anthony asked

Had each of these people been down here, forced to bond with the All-Father? Had they all been made to conform due to some war the All-Father had told the Fellowship was inevitable? Just by his very existence on that property, had Joe been complicit? "What the hell have we done?"

"Let's move," Anthony said.

Joe followed him quickly up the cellar stairs.

When they went through the door of the shed, they understood what had screamed above them. Father Castor palmed his head in anguish just in front of the tree line, letting out whimpering breaths as his robe swished side to side.

"What have you done to the All-Father?!" Castor said. "He's in pain!"

Though he was practically defenseless, Joe knew it would feel good to give Castor one good smack in the jaw. He wound up, but Anthony beat him to it.

Joe and Anthony looked from the truck to the front porch, hiding out of range from the porch light. Damn, Joe wished he had thought to bring his car keys with him. Instead, he had to crawl back into the lion's den to get them.

Joe whispered, "She's in there."

Anthony whispered back, "Why don't we just bust in the door, get our shit, and leave? Darla, she falls down hard for such a small woman."

"Did you punch her too?"

"Focus, Joe."

"Shit. Right. If they know you're out, they'll send the Fellowship after us. You know they will. My landline doesn't have any range, and she'll hear me make a call. If I can get to a phone—"

"I couldn't get a signal out here. We need to get to a far enough distance to make a call."

"I'm gonna walk in and just get the keys and my phone. When I back the truck up, I'll swing it this way. You hop in the passenger's seat. By the time they know you're gone, the cops'll be on their way."

"Can we even trust the cops here?"

"This whole town ain't part of the Fellowship, Ant."

Joe gathered himself, ready to blend in again, preparing a joyous enactment of a man proud to have his brother join the cause. Anthony touched his shoulder before he could go.

Anthony whispered, "It's good to have you back, man. I thought you were gone for good."

Truthfully, Joe felt that he had been gone for a long time, even before the worms. "There's a lot I gotta catch you up on," he said.

Joe dipped into the light, creeping toward the porch and up the stairs to the front door.

SQUIRMING ALL THE WAY UP

Darla wasn't in the living room, something that gave Joe a feeling of both relief and anxiety.

He found the keys and his cell phone on the kitchen counter where he'd left them next to the groceries, which Darla hadn't put away.

He went back to the front door, his phone and keys clasped in one hand. He opened the door ...

"You're a good man, Joe Sanderson," Darla said from behind him.

With one hand on the doorknob and the other holding his belongings, Joe peered through the cracked door at his brother hovering anticipatorily in the woods. From Anthony's vantage point, he wouldn't have been able to see what was behind Joe. Joe knew this and decided it was better for them both.

Joe thought quickly. He turned, transferring the phone to his free hand, and tossed it past the porch to the dirt, making the movement slight enough he hoped Darla wouldn't notice. He tried to mask the impact with, "I think it's done, honey," as he closed the door behind him. The hope that he'd get away with it dissipated as soon as he laid eyes on his wife.

God almighty.

From the darkened hallway, her bald head came into the light first, and behind it, a leech-like object suctioned at the back of her skull, gyrating in waves, the flesh of the thing bursting with starlight. She smiled as if experiencing a beautiful high. The All-Father had its dripping exterior wrapped once around her neck, the remainder of its long tentacle vanishing down the hallway. In her hands, she held Joe's AR-15. His favorite gun.

"But I see you've made your choice." The All-Father released itself from Darla's head, pulling strings of blood back with its teeth and floating out of view. "'I am the Alpha and Omega, the beginning and the end. I will give unto him that is a thirst of the fountain of the water of life freely ... But the fearful, and unbelieving, and the abominable, and murderers, and whoremongers, and sorcerers, and idolaters, and all liars, shall have their part in the lake, which burneth with fire and' ... Oh dear, I seem to have lost my place." She raised the AR-15, the euphoric glaze leaving her eyes.

Joe raised his hands instinctually. "Why'd you bring me into this, Darla? Did you even love me?" He had to know.

Darla's face melted with sadness. Whether it was real or genuine, Joe couldn't tell anymore. "Absolutely I do. You're exactly who I've been lookin' for my whole life. I did have to press that little whore of yours hard to give up your name and location. People are so untrusting these days. But I can be very persuasive."

That whore of yours ...

"Did you ... choose me because you knew I could conceive? Have you been tracking me since I drove to the abortion clinic?"

"The All-Father led me to that clinic, Joe. He told me it was my purpose to save the unborn and to create new life. At first, I thought the Fellowship's purpose was to destroy those evil clinics, but when that bomb didn't go off, I knew it was a sign—"

"The bomb? What did you ..." Then Joe remembered. The clinic in Virginia. The very one he had so confidently accused Tyson of attempting to bomb before he knew the young man's name. "It was you that planted the bomb?"

"Oh, I had help. What is it that you think we're doing at the church all day? Preparing for one sermon? The bombs are in the cabinets downstairs in the Bible study room. The war's comin', Joe, and we'll need to be prepared."

The cabinets downstairs, Joe thought. He was just down there, surrounded by crudely assembled explosives.

"God simply wanted to put you in front of me," Darla continued. "These choices aren't our own. He led me to you. I didn't even know you were of pure blood until the All-Father's offspring took to you. And I'm so glad they did. So very glad."

"What about the others?" Joe asked.

"Other what?"

"Other men, Darla. Men that the offspring didn't take to?"

"Why would you concern yourself with that, honey?"

"What happened to them? Have other men died just because you wanted to fuck them?"

The muzzle of the gun exploded. Darla's face was so cold above the barrel Joe didn't think the gunshot was real. No reaction. Not even a flinch.

He grabbed his side as blood flowered in his shirt. He dropped to a knee, feeling like if he hunched over, it might keep everything together. But the blood just kept coming out.

"They were made from dust," Darla said, "and to the dust they did return, as we all will. Now ... you're going to stay here while I go see to it that your brother is fixed. We'll talk about this when we're both of sound mind." She walked past Joe. "If you won't give me your seed, then your brother will have to do."

For years, Joe believed conception was living proof of God's miracle, but even he knew she was delusional to think anyone else could give her children. God hadn't punished them with the inability to conceive. It was the nature of chaos. Everything that could and could not happen converging. A cold, uncaring universe showing them how powerless they were to it.

In other words, it was random, like so many things.

Joe whimpered, "Don't," right before Darla shut the door on him.

The lowly day laborer, who had grown sunspots on his arms, used to love his church, and shunned his family, bled out, feeling his life slipping out of his side. He thought of every bad decision he made that led him to that spot on the ground.

But then he thought of Anthony and realized none of this was about him anymore. If Joe allowed himself to die tonight, it meant he allowed Anthony to die as well, not in terms of Anthony's heart stopping but in terms of his natural life being altered.

Joe had brought his brother there to save him, and goddammit, now he had a chance to save him.

Save him from those goddamn worms.

He pushed himself up off the ground.

He peeled his shirt off, fixed it into a ball, and put it on his side, pressing it against the bullet wound.

He went behind the counter and found a roll of duct tape in a drawer, then secured the shirt on his midsection with it.

Darla had taken his AR-15, and he took that personally. She knew the AR was his favorite.

He'd just have to settle for the Remington stowed away in the bedroom closet.

Their bedroom no more.

Forty-One Minutes After Deworming

Joe stumbled down the porch stairs. A fog had gone up around the woods, hanging low around his ankles. The wad of shirt, heavy and soaked through, was doing its best to keep the blood inside his skin. He held the rifle tight, squeezing it hard to remind himself he could still feel.

He bumped against a tree to steady himself.

A pale figure parted the darkness in front of him, drifting into view and disrupting the thin layer of fog.

White dress, smooth face, brown hair.

She'd come to see Joe again, but this time, Joe felt like she was there to take him away. Joe's head drooped down, his vision blurring.

When he looked back up, the brunette's face materialized into the features he remembered seeing all those months ago. She had smooth, youthful skin, her nose freckled, with rosy cheeks that seemed to balloon when she smiled.

She reached out to Joe and touched his cheek.

At some point, Joe must have fallen down, because the next moment he was lifting his head out of a pile of leaves, sucking in dirt. He picked himself up, struggling to stay upright. If he could just keep himself straight, he'd be heading in the right direction.

"Her name was Bliss," he whispered, then let out a light, pitiful laugh. The thought of the woman's face in his drowsy state battled with his will to stay awake as he trekked through the woods, the rifle colliding clumsily with the surrounding trees.

Anthony's voice echoed through the trees, becoming more clear the longer Joe stood upright. "Even if they don't find the thing down there, how many cold cases do you think they're gonna solve in that cellar?"

Joe made his steps slow and deliberate, inching his way toward them.

"You think you can ruin me? You think you can ruin the Fellowship?" Darla said, appearing through an opening in the trees, walking sideways, rifle raised, angling herself toward the backside of the shed where Anthony was hiding. "We are the First Divine," she said. "We'll live on for generations, slowly building a perfect utopia free from sin."

Joe stepped closer ...

Darla slowly rounded the corner ...

"Sounds like a drag," Anthony said from behind the shed. "You know, I never did get that hug. It's not too late for us."

Joe could hear the smile in Darla's words. "We'll be free from filth like you. Come out so we can finish your cleansing."

Joe willed all the strength he had left into his forearms, his shoulders, his hands.

He aimed.

He could live in this world without his wife or without his brother.

The choice was clear.

He stepped forward, putting weight in front of him to prepare for the recoil. A twig snapped below his feet, and Darla's bald, bloodied head turned.

Stop staring through the sights and focus on the target, Anthony had told him. *You always shot better when you trusted your form.* Joe's focus shifted through the sights to Darla. She had deceived Joe time and time again, reducing him to a meat puppet worthy of her cause, but it still made Joe sad as hell to kill her.

BANG!

Joe's aim was true. The bullet popped her forehead, causing her to jerk back as a red wave plumed from behind her skull.

Darla fell lifelessly to the ground.

Anthony slowly poked his head out from behind the shed, his eyes trained on Darla's dead body. "Holy shit."

Darla had gone down with the AR-15 still in her hands, and Joe had to make sure she wasn't going to pop up. He got close enough to see that her eyes were stuck in a forever state of surprise. Her chest failed to rise. She was dead.

Joe lowered the rifle and grabbed his side. The skin had gone numb around the wound, and he barely felt his hand push the wet rag into it. "She took the AR," he said. "She knew that was my favorite."

Joe fell to a knee, and Anthony caught him before he crumbled to the ground.

"Jesus, look at you," Anthony said. He glanced back at Darla and said, "You *are* a good shot."

"Just breakin' old habits is all."

Police sirens whined from the other side of the trees. Anthony had done it.

"We need to move," Anthony said. He propped Joe up on his shoulder and carried him through the fog.

Joe fought back sleep the entire time, the blankness in his vision trying to pull him under.

Not too long after, the flashing reds and blues sent shockwaves into Joe's vision.

Someone with blue hands shined a light in Joe's eyes.

One Hour Forty-Two Minutes After Deworming

"It would have been appropriate, I thought," Joe said, his vision starting to come back to him. "Some kind of cosmic punishment for being a shitty brother and a shitty son. In a lot of ways, though, I feel like my eyes are open and I can start fresh.

"What hurts the most is that it took you getting kidnapped by my crazy-ass wife and a conspiracy of space worms or somethin' to help me understand that this was all a big lie. It's funny, isn't it? People can scream in our faces. They can march in the streets. They can beg us to treat them like human beings. But it's not until one of your own is impacted by the evil roots you plant that you realize the problem is you.

"What I'm trying to say is, if none of this ever happened—if you never showed up to write a story about the church, if you were never drugged and thrown into a hole, if I never had the worms frozen out of me, if I never saw that wall of photographs—I'd still think you were a sinner that needed to be saved. Impurity in need of cleansing or whatever.

"I don't know what I believe in anymore. Can I just be okay with that? Do I have to know everything? You seem to be fine not knowin', but it's like the world is mysterious all over again now. Nothing fits together. Questions don't have answers. But why should they, I guess.

"I don't know if God's real or not. I'd like to believe God's real. There's nothing wrong with belief, right? I'm pretty sure, though, if I die right now, that's the end of it. I don't think I'm going to a good place or a bad place. To be honest, this place was bad enough, and it could've been good if I let it be. I also know that if I somehow make it through this, it won't be because God saved me. There's no scale that leans toward death in one direction and life in the other.

"I can choose to believe that an ancient deity governs the universe, but if I accept that, I also have to accept one hard fact. Assuming an omnipotent, all-mighty being can *feel* anything in the way you and I perceive it ...

"God is very fucking disappointed with us, huh?"

Clap clap clap.

All Joe could hear were claps, causing violent pulses through his head.

Why was Anthony clapping?

"That was quite the lovely speech." The voice wasn't Anthony. His hearing was coming back to him, becoming more clear. "Pity. All-Father won't be pleased with what you've become."

Joe fluttered his eyelids, trying to blink whoever the voice belonged to into life.

The frame of a body and a head faded into view.

"You've been corrupted beyond redemption, son," the voice said, becoming clearer. It was high-pitched. Young. There was only one person with a voice that high who called Joe son. He was twenty-two years old and had no business calling Joe that.

"Castor ..." Joe said faintly.

"You have to know this is a big disappointment to me ... to the Fellowship. He loved you like a son. And I loved you like a brother."

Joe was so weak he couldn't move. Castor was beginning to come into view before him, the scraggly-looking mustache, the shaggy brown hair, the blemish-ridden pale face. The checkered lining of a hospital ceiling was fixed above him.

"You know," Castor said, "there are some modern philosophers who believe that Christianity is an invention. That the Bible was written as a tool to control people. See, the fallacy of human beings is their awareness of existence. We believe that the things we do must have some kind of meaning. Otherwise, why the heck are we here? And if there's one idea we become obsessed with, it's the idea of virtue. But people can't just be virtuous on their own, yeah? There needs to be some incentive. *Why* am I being virtuous? You tell someone they're servin' a higher purpose, that they're *morally* superior to someone who doesn't, there's nothing they won't do to serve it ... Anyhoo, it's just a theory. If only those philosophers knew what Father Johanson found, they'd know that there *is* a higher power. The All-Father shows us the future. A future that's nearly here. And as much as I hate it, he chose you as a messenger, and I must respect his wishes. After all, he chose me too."

The hissing rose to a pitch higher than Joe had experienced, even from within his own skull.

"Anthony ..." Joe said.

"I'm not Anthony, son. I told you this."

"Anthony ... will find you."

SQUIRMING ALL THE WAY UP

"I'm sorry to tell you this, Joe, but at this point, your brother's gone. He was taken away from here. If it's any consolation, I was told it'd be quick."

"He isn't dead. I'd know it if he was."

"How do you figure?"

Joe smirked. "We have that special brother thing."

A scream came from outside the hospital door. Father Castor looked back. "It sounds like the offspring are busy." He walked over to the door and opened it.

"What did you do?" Joe asked.

Just then, Castor leaped back and a hand slapped against the frame. A woman in blue scrubs coughed up bile into the entrance, chunks of organs and rotted flesh sliding within it. She lifted her shirt and clawed at her stomach, blasting obscenities into the air. A pair of nurses grabbed her arms frantically and rushed her out of view.

"Rapid expansion," Father Castor said, his eyes on Joe. "That's my purpose."

And to the dust they shall return.

Father Castor approached Joe. "I told you. You have to keep consuming the offspring. The Fellowship had to burn the shed. That was a given. But I went down there before they did and offered to be his vessel. He let me consume so many offspring, Joe. Now I have some to spare." He leaned over Joe and opened his mouth. The hissing grew louder, like a rattlesnake inside his body.

A sloshing sound came from his throat.

A mash of energetic worms climbed onto Castor's tongue.

And spilled onto Joe's face.

CHAPTER SIX

One Hour Twenty-Nine Minutes After Deworming

"A giant fuckin' worm? Are you kiddin' me?" Officer Duffy said from the driver's seat of his police cruiser. The car reeked of cologne, and Anthony wondered why the hell he thought it was a good idea to spritz himself for the late shift.

"I saw what I saw, man," Anthony said. "I know it sounds ridiculous—"

"It sounds like you've had a very traumatic experience. Your mind must've been playin' tricks on you."

"I woke up in that dungeon chained to the wall. I was down there with that thing *twice*."

"You were drugged. You said it yourself."

"Come on, man—"

"The only person who could tell us what went into your system tonight, well ... she ain't here anymore, is she?"

Anthony was starting to feel a twist in his stomach. He wanted to be anywhere but the back seat of that car. The drive had lasted far too long, and all he'd seen were blackened trees scraping the edges of the night sky. The only person who knew where they were going was the uniformed man in front of him.

"You said it'd take twenty minutes to get to the hospital," Anthony said. "Where are we?"

"Ah, we're just about there."

The headlights flashed across a metal gate spread open between two wooden posts. Anthony felt the vehicle dip on one side as it left the asphalt and mounted a bumpy dirt road. The wooden posts faded past either side of the cruiser as it scampered down the uneven path.

Anthony felt like he was being led to slaughter. "Where are we going?" he asked.

"Tell me more about them worms," Duffy said. "Did any of 'em get on ya? ... Did they get *in* ya?"

"I thought you didn't believe me about the worms."

They drove further into a field that stretched so far the headlights couldn't shape the edges of it. It was all darkness swallowing the halos of light.

"Now," Duffy said, "you have an opportunity here to be truthful. I got to know if any of the worms got in ya." He slowed the car to a stop.

Anthony swayed with the shifting momentum of the car, hearing the brakes screech and the engine hum.

"Not sure what to say, huh?" Duffy laughed. "Let's get outta the car. Come on." He pushed open his door.

As Duffy pulled himself out of the seat, Anthony got a glimpse of the handgun on his side, flashing under the car light. Once again, he felt small, insignificant, helpless. An ant under a boot.

"Come on," Duffy said. He slammed the door shut, took a step toward the back end of the cruiser with his chest high. He tapped on the window, then opened the passenger door, nodding for Anthony to come out.

A collage of memories flooded Anthony's consciousness. Memories that didn't exist yet of the child he wouldn't have. Memories of his brother, who would never leave this place. Memories of his mother, who would've been sad as hell to know he died like this. But Anthony knew there would be no obituary for him. Duffy wasn't going to kill him in the traditional sense.

He was going to make Anthony disappear.

Anthony's hand shook against the door as he pushed it open further and stepped out slowly to face Duffy. The officer held the world's smuggest smile, feeding off the fear that Anthony couldn't possibly hide.

"Darla warned me about you," he said. "Told me you was a journalist and you was out to expose the Fellowship. That right?"

"Uh ..." No use lying about it now. "Yep, you got me."

"That's why I really gotta know if you have the offspring."

Anthony didn't speak.

"Do you have the mark?" Duffy asked.

Anthony took a moment to respond. "What mark?"

"The mark that makes you see." Duffy smiled wide and began unbuttoning his uniform, freeing a wider view of his white undershirt with each button. He gripped the collar of his undershirt and pulled it down, causing the fabric to stretch and expose his left breast. On said breast was a circle of dried blood, which could've looked like a tattoo from a distance. The skin was raised around the circle where it had tried and failed to repair itself.

"I chose to connect the All-Father to my heart," Duffy said. "If the All-Father accepted you, he would have given you the mark too. He hasn't gifted me with the visions yet, but I know he will soon. He doesn't show everyone their purpose, not right away, but I know he'll show me someday. Where's your mark?"

Anthony didn't know what to say. All he hoped for at this point was to turn the man's smile upside down and halt the momentum of his weapon before he could raise it.

"Oh yeah, the mark. He left it on my left ass cheek," Anthony said with his heart in his throat. "Would you like to see?"

He was then standing in a remote field in front of a uniformed police officer, who had his shirt unbuttoned with one breast exposed, looking like an inexperienced stripper in the middle of a sad routine. If he was going to die, it wasn't the worst thing to remember as his last image.

Duffy took a deep, disappointed breath. "I guess there's nothing else to talk about, then."

They stared each other down for what felt like minutes.

The hum of the engine drowned out, and all Anthony could hear was the beating of his heart thumping against his chest, his fingertips, his eardrums.

Duffy reached for his gun.

Anthony registered the movement too slowly, and Duffy had the pistol raised before he could react.

Anthony shielded his face with his arms, preparing for impact.

BANG!

JOEY POWELL

Anthony thought it would hurt, but it didn't.

He didn't feel a thing.

He lowered his arms, studying Duffy's puzzled face. An entry and exit wound ran from one cheek to the other. The gun dangled from Duffy's hand, remaining in a half-raised state.

BANG!

A hole formed on Duffy's forehead, and a splash of blood flicked out the back of his skull. He fell to the ground, his entire body stiff and his shooting arm at a forty-five-degree angle.

Anthony spun around with his hands up, hoping he wouldn't end up like poor, pitiful Duffy, who enjoyed getting his chest sucked and telling people about it.

The scattered sounds of an old muffler came forward. Headlights flipped on, making Anthony wince.

"It's okay!" Anthony heard over the muffler.

A station wagon came into view and stopped behind the police cruiser. The door opened, and a tall figure stepped out, striding forward in a beanie, a bomber jacket, skinny jeans, and leather boots. Anthony recognized the man's boyish face, patchy facial hair, and light-brown skin. The man had introduced himself as Tyson at the gas station the day before.

"Holy shit," Anthony said.

Tyson slung his rifle with its shoulder strap to his back. "You okay?" he said as he passed Anthony and made his way to the corpse that used to be Officer Duffy.

He poked at Dead Duffy's stomach with the toe of his boot. "Yep, he's pretty dead. Sorry it took so long. Just had to wait for him to pull his gun. Had to be sure he was one of them."

SQUIRMING ALL THE WAY UP

"Uh ... Thank you." The words were tangled in Anthony's state of shock, coming out like a question.

"Don't mention it. You took out the matriarch. The Fellowship's about to explode."

"You mean Darla?"

"One and the same. Your brother's wife."

"My brother," Anthony said. "He was in an ambulance last I saw him."

"I saw. That's good; that should get him out of the radius of influence," Tyson said. "Let's get this body in the trunk. Then we'll head to the hospital." Tyson clutched Dead Duffy's ankles, and the gun slid off his back. "Shit." He looked up at Anthony. "You gonna help me carry this guy, or what?"

Anthony snapped himself out of the fog, the light feeling in his legs subsiding as the adrenaline stopped its surge. He lifted Dead Duffy by the armpits, feeling his back strain against the weight.

They got to the back of the station wagon, and Tyson dropped the legs, then opened the hatch. The floor and the back of the seats were covered in a black tarp. At the side of the hatch sat a folded strand of thick rope, a roll of duct tape, and a folded blanket.

"Looks like a serial killer's trunk," Anthony said.

Without responding, Tyson grabbed Dead Duffy's ankles, and together, they lifted the body into the cargo area, the suspension squeaking under the mass. Tyson worked quickly, grabbing the rope and wringing it around Dead Duffy's neck, pulling it tight. He snagged a look at Anthony, seeing the confusion he wasn't good at hiding.

"I'm cutting off the blood flow to the brain," Tyson said. "It's slower, but much easier than sawing through his neck."

"Why are either of those things options? The guy's already dead."

"Yeah, but the worms aren't," he said, giving another quick yank of the rope. He tied a knot. "They thrive on living hosts, particularly on regular-to-high body temperatures. Once he goes cold, they'll be looking for new hosts."

"The worms?"

Tyson chuckled. "I guess they do look like worms, don't they?" Satisfied with his knot, Tyson grabbed the roll of duct tape and pulled a strand free, making a loud ripping sound.

"I thought they just died if they can't bond," Anthony said.

Tyson stopped. "Shit ... They're not inside you, are they?"

"No."

Tyson let out a relieved sigh. "That's only before the offspring—the 'worms'—reach maturity. From what we've seen, they can go about twenty-four hours between hosts." He began wrapping the duct tape from the bottom of Dead Duffy's chin, each new layer further concealing a dumb look of surprise—the last gesture Alive Duffy's face made before he became his dead self. "This is to make sure they don't have a place to go."

With the head completely mummified, Tyson ripped off the strand of tape and stepped back, taking a final look.

"So you've done this before?" Anthony asked, trying to peel his eyes away from the dead man with a silver head.

"Yeah," Tyson said. He grabbed the blanket wedged between the corpse and the seat and spread it over Dead Silver-Headed Duffy. "Let's get ourselves to the hospital." He pulled the hatch shut.

As they distanced themselves from the field and hit the main road, a high-pitched hissing sound came from the back of the station wagon, similar to what Anthony had heard in the cellar but higher, more intense, almost the way he would imagine a parasite screaming. The farther they drove, the louder the hissing got.

"What's that sound?" Anthony asked.

"Oh, that's the worms," Tyson said casually. "That's the sound they make when they're dying."

In a calm tone, Tyson told Anthony he'd been in the underground cellar, had seen the fuzzy VHS tape with the old man dressed in white. This led to a discussion of Viking theology and how that translated through the centuries to Christianity. Anthony knew the Vikings didn't believe in one all-powerful god. Based on Tyson's experience being forced into the cult, he said the Viking heritage was simply in service of a warrior mentality, inspiring an urge for dominance within a people who had only experienced privilege. Their theology fell out of fashion.

It could have been any religion, really. Religion was simply a delivery mechanism for spreading worms. There had to be some benefit to it. Some kind of quid pro quo that forced people to abandon their natural instincts.

"That police officer had a mark on his chest," Anthony said as they sped down the dark road. "He called it the mark that makes you see. What was he talking about?"

"Yeah, that. Certain people—not everyone—have some kind of connection to the All-Father. Or maybe he just chooses them; I don't know." Tyson was cool and collected, making Anthony wonder how many times he'd answered this same question. "The only way I can describe it is ... he puts images in their heads. They're never the same, but they seem to reflect some kind of fear or prejudice. Why do you think I was taken in?" He gave Anthony a quick glance before looking back at the road. When Anthony couldn't wager a guess, Tyson held up his hand and waved it in front of Anthony's face. "I'm a darker shade than they are. A *slightly* darker shade, but dark enough for some hillbilly in the most backwoods parts of Virginia to notice. I was kidnapped by a man who said he was told by God that mixing the races was destroying traditional American values, whatever that means. But instead of killing me, he wanted to convert me. Thought that maybe through a couple generations of proper breeding, they could weed out my non-whiteness."

Traditional American values, Anthony thought. Three words carried such a heavy charge, bursting at the seams of rationality within the psyche of the man who said them. The irony of the story was that Anthony understood the actions, not the rationale, to a true reflection of traditional American values.

Anthony understood that America was built on theft and imposition.

Some things never change.

"My theory is," Tyson continued, "the All-Father preserves itself by adapting to prejudice. If you believe in that story of the Viking tribe and all that, well ... the Vikings weren't a noble people. They pillaged, they raped, they enslaved. They dominated. They reigned supreme because of their cruelty."

They grew because they were savages, Anthony thought.

One Hour Forty-Three Minutes After Deworming

Something was wrong. Anthony could feel it.

The station wagon came to a stop at the farthest edge of the hospital parking lot. The stench from Duffy's body had wafted all the way to Tyson and Anthony, tickling their nostrils with putrid whiffs of death.

The overhead lights of the parking lot struck daggers through Tyson's dirty windshield, illuminating lines of vehicles.

Anthony clutched the door handle, ready to sprint straight through the entrance.

"Try not to draw attention to yourself," Tyson said. "Remember what we have in here."

The automatic doors opened on the other side of the lot.

Anthony and Tyson watched as a man ran frantically onto the sidewalk, his back arched, holding his stomach like he was worried it would fall out. A mixture of shrill cries and grunts exited his lungs as he began to stumble.

"Shit," Tyson said. He flew out the driver's side door, ignoring his own advice, and dashed toward the man.

Anthony did the same, hearing Tyson mumble, "No, no, no."

The pained man dropped to his knees, his thinning hair matted with sweat, looking at Anthony and Tyson with frightened eyes. Black trails glistened under the fluorescent lights—a web of grime coalescing at the man's mouth.

"Help," the man said gently. His stomach stirred.

Anthony bent down to help him, but Tyson halted Anthony with an arm.

The man's insides fell through his skin like a smashed tank of water, soaking through his shirt. The black rot that was once his midsection spilled onto the sidewalk. Air escaped his lungs, and the man fell into the rot.

"Offspring," Tyson said.

Another scream traveled from inside the building.

Anthony bolted into the hospital, squeezing through the automatic door and into the lobby.

The hospital was in absolute chaos.

Black lines of residue zigzagged around the lobby and the front desk. A security officer slapped at his shoulder, flinging a worm off, and waddled farther into the hospital, running toward the screams. A flurry of white coats and scrubs appeared and disappeared from room to room, floor to floor.

A worm slid along the once-polished lobby floor next to Anthony. He smashed it with his heel.

"Anthony, we don't even know where he is!" Tyson yelled behind him, but there was no stopping Anthony now.

He rushed through corridor after corridor, following the overhead arrows leading to the Emergency Room, past wide-eyed workers reacting to the sickness that was spreading through the hospital, past the piles of stomach rot and lifeless bodies ripped open on the floor, past walls smeared in black lines like streaks of fingerpaint.

He grabbed a woman in a white coat by the collar. "Joe Sanderson! He's a patient! Do you know where he is?!"

SQUIRMING ALL THE WAY UP

The woman slipped free, her face a panicked mess, speaking so fast he could barely understand her. "Sir, we have a contagion spreading. I suggest you find a room and stay in it." She ran past him.

Anthony kept running.

Until he slid into a hallway, coming to a stop as he stared ahead at a young man in a robe at the other end, his arms behind his back, standing still.

Castor.

Stirs of grunts and struggle sprang from the open door next to the pastor.

"Anthony Sanderson," he said with his long Southern drawl. "Mighty nice to officially meet you."

Anthony stomped forward. "Where's my brother?"

"He's currently fulfillin' his destiny. I'm gonna have to ask ya not to interfere."

Anthony picked up the pace. "Didn't you hear? It's what I'm good at." He charged forward.

The pastor opened his mouth wide, hurling a flood of worms at Anthony like spray from a can.

Anthony held an arm to block them, feeling the wet sludge punch against his skin, then tackled Castor, who spewed another wave of worms upward, missing Anthony's face. Anthony balled his fist and punched the pastor's neck, forcing him to gag and clutch his throat.

Something danced inside Anthony's mouth. He repositioned it with his tongue and chomped, then spat the remnants in Castor's face.

He turned his head to the open room, where Joe, wearing a hospital gown, slapped at his skin, shaking his head. Joe ripped the blood bag out of his forearm, sending a trail of blood to the floor.

"Joe!" Anthony yelled.

Joe shook the worms out of his hair and stood woozily off the bed, a layer of squirming worms covering him. He winced, and his hands flew to his side.

Anthony ran to him and swatted at the worms, dropping what must have been two dozen. He stomped them out until there were none left squirming in his sight.

He put a shoulder under Joe, holding him up.

"What took you so long?" Joe said.

"Got tied up. Can you run?"

"No."

"Well, you're gonna have to."

"Where's Castor?"

Anthony looked out through the door frame. The boyish man in dramatic black and white fabric was gone.

Tyson slid into view, panting, eyes wide. "Shit, you found him," he said, surprised. He took a breath. "Nice job. Quickly now." He made a waving motion, directing them his way.

Anthony helped Joe out of the room, following Tyson down the corridor and into the symphony of screams.

"What do we do about this?!" Joe yelled weakly at Tyson's back. "We have to help these people!"

"We can't do anything!" Tyson responded. "They're everywhere, and it won't be long before this place gets locked down!" Tyson juked past a black missile of vomit dispersed by a patient as she punched her stomach, taking her last breaths.

"Let's just focus on getting our asses out!" Anthony yelled.

SQUIRMING ALL THE WAY UP

They took the stairs, which were devoid of the black slime that stained the hallways. Tyson and Anthony worked together to lower Joe down the stairs as he winced and grunted with every painful step.

"We have to help them. We have to help them. We have to go back," Joe muttered to himself.

He had to have known it was useless. The worms had claimed their hosts and rejected many, many more.

Tyson led them through a side exit with his car waiting on the other side. Sirens howled as soon as they opened the door.

"How'd you know to park here?" Anthony asked.

"One look inside and I knew the place was going to be quarantined."

They rushed Joe into the backseat, careless as to how the motions would impact his stitches. The grunts and whines let Anthony know that the stitches were pulling at his skin. "I'm sorry, bro," Anthony said, which was the only tenderness he had time to express.

Anthony flew into the passenger seat and felt the station wagon shake with Tyson's presence shortly thereafter. The engine roared to life.

"Oh my god, did something die in here?" Joe said from the backseat, coughing on the stench.

Anthony and Tyson glanced at each other. Neither answered.

"What the hell was all that?" Anthony said, forcing himself to blink. The thought had crossed his mind that maybe his eyes would stay this wide forever until someone took the rough end of a sponge and scrubbed the images from the hospital out of his brain.

Having just barely evaded the response vehicles, the inhabitants of which would surely have no idea what the hell they were actually responding to, Anthony felt the come-down of adrenaline as he gazed ahead at the dark road before him, listening to the hum of the tires.

"It's what happens when the offspring don't bond with a host," Tyson said. His voice was shaking, his hands rattling against the wheel. The confident marksman Anthony had first met was still in the parking lot of that hospital. "I'd only seen it happen once before tonight. All those people ..." Tyson's hands squeezed the steering wheel, creating a loud squeak of friction. "They didn't have a choice. Just like I didn't."

"Just like Trisha didn't," Anthony said, grinding his teeth. Meer hours ago, Anthony was sitting across the table from a kid who'd had her life altered *for* her. A kid who liked to write and dabbled in spooky shit. Knowing that the actions of the Fellowship could have resulted in a painful episode of violent spasms, in her feeling her insides rapidly decay and her body failing her, that her last image could have been the reverse side of her stomach on the ground, made him want to punch a hole in the dash.

"How was she when you saw her?" Tyson asked.

"She was having stomach pains," Anthony said. "Practically crawling on the ground asking if what she was feeling was normal."

Tyson let out a satisfied sigh, sounding like it was the only good news he'd ever heard. "Then she still has some autonomy."

"What do you mean?" Anthony knew Trisha was there behind that glassy stare. She was buried behind a coffin, pounding from the inside, trying to get out.

"It takes a while for the worms to burrow inside a host's brain," Tyson said. "Before that, they don't have much control over your brain chemistry. They likely used some brainwashing methods to help make her complacent till the worms take hold, but she's still able to call the shots. For now at least."

A rustle of fabric preceded a groan as Joe sat up. "We have to go to the church."

The suggestion caused Anthony's chest to tighten. The last place he wanted to be was in a place of worship. "We have to lay low and let you rest, Joe."

"They built the church on top of the All-Father," Joe said.

But Anthony had seen the All-Father rear its ugly alien head through the hole in the underground cellar. Did it simply exist in the underbelly of South Point, forcing its way around like sludge through cracks in the bedrock of the ground the citizens lived on? Had the Fellowship built a tunnel system to allow it to travel unnoticed?

"You've seen it there?" Tyson asked.

"Up close and personal," Joe said softly, sounding like he might pass out at any moment.

Anthony watched Tyson stare down the road ahead and bear his teeth angrily like a wolf ready to strike. "Then let's kill the damn thing," Tyson said.

"How?" Anthony interjected. "It's an alien that squirts out worms. What do we do about the people that are already infected?"

"When I chopped it with the pickaxe, it was like the worms were affected by it," Joe said. "You were there. You saw it."

Then Anthony remembered the way the giant worm screeched like a fork being dragged across a plate, how it cowered back inside its hole like a wounded animal. He remembered the pissant hovering around the shed yelping and grabbing his head as if trying to hold it together. Anthony was scared shitless and therefore didn't want to admit that Joe was probably right.

But Tyson did it for him. "It makes sense. The All-Father needs hosts to maintain its life force."

"You don't know what it's like, Anthony," Joe said. "You don't know what it's like to have them in your head. To have so much hate festering inside y—"

"Are you *listening* to yourselves?!" A burst of frustration or fear or insanity fled from Anthony's mouth. For all he knew, the images drilled into his brain were figments of his imagination. They were pure impossibilities. Things that existed in the nightmares of children. "We don't even know what the thing is. How are we supposed to ..." He was beyond frightened by what he'd seen. He only barely came out of this situation unscathed and saw no reason to throw himself back in. "How are we supposed to kill it?"

"Bombs," Joe said. "The church is fully stocked with them."

"No shit?" Tyson said in surprise.

"We just keep peeling back layer after wholesome layer of this church, don't we, Joe?" Anthony said. "Bombing a church. That'll be great PR."

"We don't bomb *the church*," Joe said. "The All-Father's underground. We place the bombs above the All-Father and bury it. Here's what we do ..."

As Joe continued talking, his voice rose from a weakling's whisper from their deathbed to a man determined to go to war. There was such confidence to Joe's voice and demeanor that he was beginning to believe it might actually work. There were so many what-ifs to the plan, the least of which being whether they'd be met with any resistance from members of the church. Did they congregate at night to have a cosmic circle jerk and talk about how much they loved each other and hated everyone else?

But on the microscopic chance that it would, it may have been a chance for Anthony to do some real good. So much of his adult life had been dedicated to keyboard activism, exploiting people he knew were bad to give the media machine bogeymen to be mad at, to hate. Something for any random person to share on social media with a barrage of expletives and diatribes regarding the end of civilization as we all know it, then forget about the next day as they went about their boring, uneventful lives.

And if they did this—if they succeeded and somehow didn't blow themselves up—no one would ever know about it. Anthony would go hunting an intergalactic worm, free minds, and any written record would be reserved for a science fiction paperback. There would be no content, no scathing takedown of a cult, no marketing campaign for what Joe was suggesting they do.

Anthony had been pulled into South Point due to his brother's righteous quest for virtue, only for his brother to now present him with one instead.

Joe's hand touched his shoulder. "I don't want this family reunion to end, brother."

Even though it was cheesy as hell, Anthony was touched. "Okay, fine." He put his hand over Joe's. "Let's blow up a god."

CHAPTER SEVEN

To Kill a Worm

There's something eerie about a church at night, Joe thought. *The whole story of Christianity is a battle of good against bad, light against dark. So much of the scripture involves darkness. So much of the mythology involves devils and demons, sin and temptation. To enter a church in the daytime is to enter a place of good, with sunlight distorted by windows of brightly colored tapestries.*

But to see the church sitting in the dark with a thumbnail's glow of moonlight barely outlining a giant cross was like seeing good stripped away from a house of peace, throwing it into chaos. The feeling shouldn't have been so foreign to him, he thought, considering every good thing he once knew about the Fellowship was one unscalable mountain of bullshit. The pain clawing at his side reminded him of that with every breath.

Anthony was quick to remind Joe that the Fellowship had made a dud. How could they even verify whether the bombs were legit? But Joe reminded him that bombs were explosives. All they needed to do was set them on fire.

Probably. Joe wasn't exactly an explosives expert.

Tyson had a tube for fuel siphoning in the way, way back of the station wagon. He traveled a lot, and the places he traveled to, well, sometimes they didn't have gas stations close by. Anthony suggested just blowing up the car so they could get rid of the body in the back and set off the bombs all at once, but then realized it would leave them stranded at a crime scene, and that was the last suggestion he made.

With the church within their view, Joe instructed the others to sit tight and watch him closely. He would go out to the field at the side of the church and show them his best estimate of where the All-Father's cave was underneath. "If you can leak the gas in a circle around it," Joe said, "Anthony can bring out the bombs and place them in the circle. You got a lighter?"

"Sure do," Tyson said.

"We light the gas on fire and—boom—bury the All-Father."

Anthony bobbed his head, considering the plan. "It's actually ... not a bad plan," he said.

Maybe he'd just succumbed to the madness of the situation, relinquishing any good sense he had before to run away from South Point back to his cozy apartment and keyboard and never come back. But Joe was happy to be with him now. Happy to be having conversations that didn't have to deal with "what" Anthony was or whom he chose to love. If they made it through this, he would love to see the life Anthony created in Minneapolis.

Joe should have been upset. He could've cursed Anthony for using him as a subject in a tasteless article of small-town groupthink and how religion is rotting the core of the country or whatever. But how could he in good conscience be upset? He didn't know much about journalism, but he could guess that Anthony had come to South Point with a theory, and every anecdote he jotted down was all in service of strengthening that theory.

What had Joe done if not proven him right?

"But what happens if we don't kill it?" Anthony said. "What happens if we just piss it off?"

"Let's just hope that doesn't happen," Joe said.

"I'll start siphoning," Tyson said. He held up a fist to both Joe and Anthony, his knuckles facing each of them. "Let's do this, boys."

It was a completely unironic gesture only a kid his age would make, and Joe would have laughed if he thought the motion wouldn't tug at his wound.

Anthony shrugged and gave him a fist bump. "Whatever. Let's be good people, I guess."

Joe did the same. "If anyone from the Fellowship's in there—and who knows if they will be—I'll try to distract them as long as I can and give y'all enough time to set the bombs up."

"Don't try to be a damn hero," Anthony said. "If you think you need some grand redemption, just wipe that shit from your brain now. We got ourselves a clean slate. Don't go dicking around and screw that up."

Anthony couldn't have known what his words meant to Joe in that moment. If he were being honest, Joe would have said his body didn't feel up for this. It begged for the comfort of that hospital bed again, his eyes refusing to stay open. But Anthony had just said they had a clean slate. He had to see that through.

"He's right," Tyson said. "We're all making it out of this. Deal?"

Joe nodded.

Tyson unholstered a revolver and held it out to Anthony. "Take this."

"Nope, not for me," Anthony said, holding his hands up.

Same old Anthony, Joe thought. Even in a time of crisis, he stuck to his principles.

"Give it here." Joe swiped it from Tyson. Instinctively, he reached down to put the barrel in his waistband around his kidney but remembered he was still wearing a dumb hospital gown. "Anyone got a fresh pair of pants?"

"Not unless you wanna undress Officer Duffy back there."

And that was the end of that.

Joe pulled himself out of the station wagon, feeling a faint summer breeze climbing up his ass cheeks through the thin fabric. He walked over to his best approximation of the All-Father's dungeon. He limped pitifully, found his spot, and spun himself around in a circle with his shooting arm extended, marking a circle for the gasoline with the barrel of the revolver.

Tyson walked out and handed him a flashlight, leaving Joe with no empty hands. "Careful in there."

"Careful of what?" Joe said. "These're my people." He grinned.

Anthony approached from behind Tyson. "Just tell me when the coast is clear and I'll get to work."

The church doors were unlocked. Joe slid right in, trying to hide his limp with every step. The stabbing pain at his side seemed like it was a part of him now, as annoying and perpetual as an achy back, and he wondered if he risked not ever having it heal.

He came to the stage and looked around the dark room. He turned back to the doors, seeing Anthony's head poking through. He gave his brother a thumbs-up, then made his way to the back door. It, too, was unlocked.

A sound like moaning grew as Joe went down the stairs, stepping closer to flickering candlelight.

There in the Bible study room, surrounded by two walls of lit candelabras, stood a group of followers with their heads raised, a pulsating black arm attached to each of them, covering heads, necks, stomachs, mouths. The arms twisted like spilled ink suspended in air, leading back to the open dungeon door. The followers grunted and whimpered blissfully. If Joe didn't have the ability to see, he would've guessed it was an orgy.

Though it was dark, he could make out the large figure of Father Henry, an eighty-year-old man who wore the evidence of his age on his sagging skin, standing in the middle of the group with a black arm attached to his stomach. The small figure of Trisha McCann stood next to him with an arm suctioned to her side. No one seemed to realize Joe was there. All eyes were to the ceiling.

Joe tried to peel his eyes away from the ghastly sight, the black arms interwoven like wires on a fuse box, tensing, then going just a little bit limp before tensing again. What was the All-Father pumping into them? Was it really just images?

What were they seeing?

Joe looked down past the red spillage marking his wound at the revolver shining in the light of flames, wondering what he'd do next.

"Warning shot," Anthony said with an uncertain breath, sounding as scared as Joe felt.

JOEY POWELL

Between the state of his body and the state of his mind, Joe was frozen stiff. The gun suddenly felt heavy, as if it would fall from his hand.

He didn't have to worry about that, though, because Anthony ripped the gun out of his grip. A shot clapped against the ceiling.

The group screamed, broken from their daze.

Joe turned back to Anthony, who had the gun raised high.

"We don't have all night, Joe," Anthony said. He shoved Joe out of the way, and Joe felt his side pull apart a little more with the sudden motion.

Joe watched as Anthony waved the gun around the room, mimicking some version of a badass. The gun looked strange in his hand, only because Joe knew Anthony had never wanted it to be there in the first place.

"Get out! All of you!" Anthony stepped aside from the basement entrance and nudged the barrel toward it. "Let's go!"

Father Henry laughed. "My boy. Are you really going to massacre us in a church?"

Joe looked from Father Henry to Trisha. Her eyes were wide in fear or pain or some combination of both as an arm of the All-Father suckled at her side, wiggling up and down. "You okay, Trisha?" Joe asked.

The arm was still attached to her side, pulsing, as she spoke. "I can feel them in my ribs," she whimpered.

"We'll get them out," Joe said.

Father Henry stepped in front of Trisha, dragging the black arm with him and causing it to slap a wad of black slime against Trisha's face. "We belong here, son," Father Henry said. "Just like you."

SQUIRMING ALL THE WAY UP

A thought sparked in Joe's head. Henry was right—they weren't going to shoot anybody. For all Joe knew, these people could still be saved. "Anthony," Joe said. "Test my theory."

"What?"

"Look at me."

Anthony did. It was that kind of look they shared when they were younger. A look that made Joe know Anthony was hearing him on a deeper level.

"Test ... my ... theory," Joe said.

Somehow, Joe knew that Anthony understood in the way his eyes squinted, looking like they were nodding in place of his head.

Anthony took three quick steps to the nearest follower, lowered the revolver to the All-Father's arm, and fired.

The eruption of the gunshot was nothing compared to the sustained screech that shot up from the dungeon through the basement, mixing with the screams of worms inside the followers' heads. The All-Father's arms broke their suction, flapping strings of blood across the room, onto the followers, onto the walls, onto Anthony and Joe. The followers grabbed their heads in unison, wailing as the worms pushed against the insides of their heads feverishly.

"Get them out!" Trisha yelled, clutching her ribs.

"Let's go! I won't say it again!" Anthony yelled as the followers fled the room, thrashing their heads back and forth, side to side. One by one, they scampered up the stairs as the arms retracted back into the dungeon.

Until only Father Henry and Trisha remained.

A scream shot from under the dungeon. "Who has hurt my worms?! Who has caused my children pain?!"

Castor.

"This way, child," Father Henry said, one hand on his head, the other clutching Trisha's arm, ignoring the commotion. "Go to Father Castor. He'll show us the way. He's the future of the Fellowship. He won't let them destroy us." He pulled Trisha toward the open dungeon door.

"Your mom says hi," Joe said. He watched Trisha's eyes tilt in sadness. "She says she wants you to paint the canvas of your world however you'd like. Somethin' like that. I'm probably not makin' sense. I've … I've lost a lot of blood, I think." He could see the wheels spinning in her head. Some part of her was hearing him.

"There's a lot of noise goin' on in your head now, right?" Joe asked, stepping closer to her, his voice trembling. "It's like a jackhammer in your skull. Somethin' telling you to judge. To hate. Feels like it's consumin' you."

A tear ran down her cheek as she resisted Father Henry's strength.

"The Fellowship forced you to be somethin' different," Joe said. "But your mom knows people who can help. She's lookin' for you."

"There's nothing to help!" Father Henry yelled. "Come with me, child!"

"I had the worms too," Joe said. "I don't anymore."

Trisha ripped her arm from Father Henry's hand, gazing at Joe solemnly.

"Let us help you."

Father Henry let out an annoyed breath. "Enough of this."

Trisha turned to him and must have seen the same golden opportunity that Joe did. Father Henry had placed himself directly under the open doorway. A man his size falls hard. Trisha gave her best push, causing him to tumble uncontrollably down the steps.

The shrieks of the All-Father grew louder from the bottom of the stairwell.

Anthony grabbed Trisha and pulled her away from the opening. She ran up the stairs and out of Joe's view.

Joe ran to the door frame and clicked on the flashlight.

Worms lined the steps and walls like rats in a sewer, inching their way up to Joe as Father Henry plummeted. "What is happening?!" Castor's angry voice echo from the dungeon. "Somebody tell me?!"

He turned back to Anthony. "Keep this door closed."

"Don't even think about it."

"I'll get myself out. I swear I will. Trust me on this, if that's even possible for you now."

Joe took the gun from Anthony and searched through the cabinets until his eyes landed on what they'd come for.

Pipe bombs. "Damn, there really are bombs in here." He tucked one under his armpit and ran back to the dungeon door.

He shined the light back down the stairwell, illuminating Castor as he hovered on the steps, worms dripping from his nose, his ears, eyes black, with pulsating arms funneling into his stomach, his back, his sides, propelling him upward.

Joe raised the gun and fired, catching Castor in the chest. Castor shrieked in an inhuman way. Joe fired at his chest again, but Castor continued his ascent toward Joe.

Joe turned to Anthony as he collected as many pipe bombs as could fit in his arms. "Close this door behind me." He braced himself for what he was about to do, an action that was sure to reopen his side completely, but he knew that was the least of his worries. He dropped the flashlight and clutched the bomb and the gun. No matter what happened, he wouldn't let them go. "Fuck it." He took one step, then another, then launched himself downward into Castor, catching the pastor in his grip. Entangled, they rolled down the steps, crunches of bone tracing their path, their bodies catching the tentacles of the All-Father, causing them to flop awkwardly in every direction. Joe's side was open again. No amount of adrenaline could keep the pain at bay. The stone steps were unforgiving, cutting through his flesh until the pain was distributed evenly across his body.

His movement finally stopped.

He lay there for a moment, face down against the warm stone, wondering what was broken and what wasn't, questioning whether every bone in his body had been turned to powder. He moved one leg, sliding his knee across the ground. He wiggled his toes on the other foot. *Good. At least my legs work.*

Something pressed against his mouth, tickling his bottom lip. He opened his eyes to see a flood of worms so close it was blurry in his vision. The horseshoe of dungeon fire created a sheen on their wet skin as they slithered, rolled, and slid.

Two worms found their way into Joe's mouth. He considered letting them in, just giving up and letting the ceiling crash down on him.

But he'd come too far. He'd gone through too goddamn much to die like this, drowning in a pool of churning worm flesh.

He'd die someday, but not like this.

Joe collected the worms with his tongue and spat them out. He lifted his head and felt a sharp sting in his spine as he pushed himself off the ground. His squeal was silenced by the sight of Father Henry's contorted body laying at the bottom of the stairs. The man lay with his chest to the ground and his head twisted in the wrong direction, his wide, dead eyes facing the ceiling.

At least Joe had better luck with the fall than he did.

Worms crowded Joe's hands, running over his fingers and bringing him to the realization that he'd lost the gun and the bomb on the way down. He shook his hands free of the worms, but they were everywhere, crawling over themselves on the stone floor, moving across the walls and toward the ceiling, spewing out that high-pitched hiss. The arms of the All-Father thrashed angrily as well, a dozen twisting, black, starry streaks swaying rapidly from the bottom of the pit beyond the fire.

Joe stood painfully and felt the worms against his ankles like an ocean wake.

A high-pitched voice shrieked from behind Joe. "What's going on?"

Joe turned to see Castor, who looked like a broken version of himself, spread out at the far edge of the circle under the fire, one leg bent to the side in a way it shouldn't have been. He breathed deep, agonizing breaths as the bullet wounds Joe had placed on his chest sprouted worms like ants evacuating an anthill. A slew of black arms slid down his back, onto his stomach, and around his sides, pulling him off the ground. He screamed as his body cracked seemingly everywhere.

Floating off the ground, his face turned upward with white puss smeared across his cheeks, he said. "Whoever is down here with me ... let the children in." Joe watched as Castor's eyes vomited worms and realized his eyes hadn't gone black; they'd popped.

"They'll show you everything," Castor said.

JOEY POWELL

The visions of Joe's mother became clear to him. She hadn't snuck his way into his mind to haunt him. She was giving him a warning, preparing him for a moment like this.

The worms crawled up Joe's neck and his mouth. He couldn't keep them out. He gasped for air as they flooded his throat. All he could do was swallow them down just to breathe, feeling them slide down his esophagus.

He gagged. "To hell with you and your worms, Castor."

Castor's cheek rose. "Joe Sanderson. So good to have you with me again, son."

Joe's eyes landed on the crudely assembled bomb, a short cylinder on the ground with worms crawling over it, then the revolver, both previously hidden from his sight by Henry's body.

"You let them take your eyes, Castor!" Joe yelled over the hissing. "Why?!"

"It's a foolish question, son," Castor coughed out his annoying, childish laugh. "It's a simple answer, though. When you know the truth, you no longer need eyes to see with."

But since Castor didn't have eyes to see with, he didn't notice Joe put the bomb at his feet. Since the hissing of the worms was so loud, he couldn't trace Joe's movements back to the steps. He couldn't see Joe aim the revolver at the bomb.

Joe didn't know the blast radius of the bomb. All he could do was hope he was far enough away, standing at one edge of the circle and aiming at the other.

His finger tightened against the trigger.

The hissing flushed away from his ears.

His mother appeared next to him. No longer was she a nightmarish ghoul with missing eyes. She was smiling warmly like a forgotten memory, filling in the gaps from fragments of a person he once knew.

For too long, Joe hated his mother for choosing Anthony over him. Seeing her, then seeing the drooping, flooded eye sockets of Castor, he realized he'd been visited by a blinded version of her before. He never needed to save her because she didn't need saving. It was *him* who needed his mother's eyes to see with.

The truth.

That was the only rational explanation he could conjure as he squeezed the trigger.

CHAPTER EIGHT

Bombs Away

Dripping sweat and sucking air, Anthony placed the last pipe bomb carefully on the ring of gasoline. The smell sat heavy in his nostrils and on his clothes. Taking a step back, he eyed his work. After four trips in and out of the church, eighteen bombs in total circled a nearly fifteen-foot radius of grass. It had to be more than enough.

What the hell were they planning with these? Anthony thought. If he were to rid the world of the Fellowship's amateur bomb assembly, he couldn't think of a better way to do it.

"You'll burn in Hell, you heathen!" The followers who fled the basement had formed a half-circle around Tyson, who leaned against his elbows on the hood of his station wagon, rifle at the ready. The sons of bitches were dumb, but Anthony didn't think they were willing to risk their lives by jumping in front of a bullet.

Not yet at least.

The frenzied headaches had appeared to subside, and all that was left were angry Christians, spitting and bobbing and yelling.

SQUIRMING ALL THE WAY UP

All except Trisha, who stood statuesque in the vibrating crowd.

An explosion shook the ground below Anthony, nearly sending him to his knees. He looked back at the church. "Joe, what did you do?"

He sprinted through the double doors, into the back room. He flung open the dungeon door, hearing the loud screech of worms.

"Joe?!" he yelled.

A cough sounded from the bottom of the stairs.

The wobbling figure of Joe came into view, halfway up the steps, backlit by the fire at the bottom of the stairwell. Screaming worms crunched with every heavy step.

Anthony went down the steps as fast as he could, forcing his lungs to spread a bit wider, carelessly mashing worms against the soles of his shoes. "How many times am I gonna have to save your stubborn ass?!" he yelled.

Joe didn't respond as his limbs wiggled upward.

Anthony put his hands against Joe's back and pushed, forcing him to pick up the pace.

"Anthony? Can you hear me? I can't ..." Joe mumbled to himself. The blast must've blown out his eardrums—temporarily, Anthony hoped.

As they made their way out of the dungeon, gunshots echoed outside the church.

"Shit ..." Anthony heaved. "What now?"

He led Joe up from the basement to the stage area. "Stay here."

"What?!" Joe yelled.

"Stay..." *Heave.* "Here!" *Heave.* "And keep away ..." *Heave.* "From the glass!"

157

Anthony ran out the doors to see a mob surrounding Tyson, wrestling the rifle from his hands. They threw fists and feet, raining hell on Tyson in a way Anthony knew he couldn't survive if it lasted too long. Then he lost the rifle in the crowd.

"Hey!" Anthony felt that all the breath in his lungs had gone.

Trisha swam forward through the crowd, a metal lighter in her hand.

Her eyes met Anthony's.

She flipped the lighter open.

"Trisha! What are you doing?!" a frantic voice called out from the crowd. Who was it? Anthony couldn't give a shit.

A flame popped out of the lighter, soaking Trisha's face in red.

Anthony nodded.

Trisha dropped the lighter and ran.

The fire rose over the grass and sprinted toward the side of the church. With his palms pressed against his ears, he waited ...

A flurry of cracks broke the silence, like fireworks on the Fourth of July. Anthony felt a shockwave ripple through his chest.

He slowly peered out from behind the church.

A hole in the earth widened with clods of falling dirt within the radius that they had placed the bombs. A scream erupted from beneath the hole. Anthony watched as a line of worms trickling from the front steps of the church thrashed violently against the brick—slapping, slapping, slapping—until they stopped moving altogether.

CHAPTER NINE

Gone the Fellowship

There were many things Joe Sanderson wished to say to his brother, but his insides felt like they'd been rearranged, shifted left and right and upside down. The bullet wound was ripped clean open and bleeding again, but he couldn't feel it. Everything was numb.

He couldn't hear very well, but there had almost certainly been an explosion outside. He hoped his plan had worked. Maybe he could leave this planet on a high note. Lord knows he'd made one giant mess of things.

A shape came toward him at a speed he couldn't perceive. Everything was going blurry now. He hoped it wasn't another ghost. It would be a real bummer to have that be his last image. *I've had enough ghosts for a lifetime*, he thought. *Let me stay here with the living.*

But the lines and colors in front of him coalesced into the face of Anthony, and thank goodness they did, because he really needed to tell his brother something. He opened his mouth to speak, but his eardrums were so shot he didn't know if the sound came out.

Anthony, I didn't know about the goddamn worms.

Anthony nodded as splotches of black replaced his face in Joe's vision. Anthony said, "I know." And then, "It worked."

Hell yeah.

Joe wished their mom could see them together again. Would she even believe it? As Joe felt his body go limp and he felt his consciousness surrender to the darkness, he found himself thinking she would. No matter the circumstances, their mother only wanted them to be together. He knew she would have crawled through Heaven and Hell to make that happen.

If this was Joe's final moment, he could go knowing she'd brought them back together. Maybe he'd see her again soon.

Then again, he'd already beaten death once.

Acknowledgements

Squirming All the Way Up has existed in some form for about five years. A lot has happened in that time, both personally and the in the world at large. I'm over the moon that there are people who believed in this book enough to publish it, but horrified that the themes within it are even more relevant today than they were five years ago. Regardless, I have some very important people to acknowledge, so, here we go ...

I honestly didn't know if this book would ever get published. Somehow, in a bit of right-time-right-place serendipity, it found a home with Madness Heart Press as part of their open call for antifascist horror. I am forever grateful to John Baltisberger at Madness Heart for including this book in a lineup filled with many talented authors, as well as Lisa Tone, the editor for this novella, for making it the best version it could be.

Thank you to Mae Murray for providing extremely crucial feedback before this manuscript was ever in the querying stage. As a developmental editor, she's worth any amount of money she asks for.

Thank you to my always-alpha-reader Josh Powell, who read a much sadder version of this this book and suggested I ease up a bit. Hope you enjoyed the worms.

Thank you to Kathy Messina, my mother, who dared me to question and speculate.

Thank you to my wife, Amanda, who is always the first to hear my strange ideas (whether she wants to or not).

Thank you to Angela Sylvaine, J.V. Gachs, David Washburn, and T.T. Madden, who are all real-life heroes and just so happened to provide awesome blurbs for this book.

And thanks to you, the reader, for sticking it out and making it this far. May you keep it weird and love unconditionally.

About the Author

Joey Powell lives on the East Coast of the United States with his wife, child, and many animals. He is Owner and Operator of Mad Axe Media, a small publisher of adult thrillers and YA nostalgia horror. In addition to being a devout consumer and creator of things spooky and weird, Joey has acted in several award-winning short films.

Find him on Instagram as @wowcooljoeywrites.

www.ingramcontent.com/pod-product-compliance
Ingram Content Group UK Ltd.
Pitfield, Milton Keynes, MK11 3LW, UK
UKHW010723070825
7249UKWH00013B/120